CROCODILE RESCUE!

MELISSA CRISTINA MÁRQUEZ

SCHOLASTIC INC.

This book is being published simultaneously in hardcover by Scholastic Press.

ISBN 978-1-338-63505-8

10 9 8 7 6 5 4 3 21 22 23 24 25

Printed in the U.S.A. 40

First printing 2021

Book design by Yaffa Jaskoll

To you.

You are worthy of being seen and included in every adventure you want to embark on, just as you are.

PROLOGUE

The camera crew faded away in slow motion, my hands clawing at the sand, desperately trying to latch on to a rock. The underwater lights disappeared into the inky darkness as I was pulled farther underwater.

Whatever you do, A, don't move that leg! screamed my inner voice as my fingers continued to rake through the mangroves' silty bottom, hoping to grab hold of a sturdy root.

Would I ever see my parents again?

Would I ever go on another adventure with Feye?

Who would take care of Duke?!

I took a quick glance back and tried not to cry as I realized how much trouble I was in: The ten-foot American crocodile had my leg firmly in its mouth.

CHAPTER ONE

"Adrianna! Feye! Come meet us in the lobby," Mom shouted over the intercom.

I was busy reapplying a bandage to Rowan's paw. The injured lion cub was the newest member at the zoo. Rowan was usually fidgety, but after we played a game of tug-of-war, he quieted down enough to let me fix the bandages he had muddied during his run around the zoo's outdoor enclosure. The squeak of a door alerted Rowan to company, and the cub quickly scurried away from my lap and tried to hide in a corner. After having been kidnapped by poachers in the wild, he was still afraid of most humans.

With a frown, I turned to the door. My older brother leaned against the frame. "Mom texted me, too," Feye said. "That new producer is on his way over to tell us more about where we're going."

I stood up, about to respond, when an automated message interrupted my thoughts. "Thank you for visiting Sacred Sanctuary and Zoological Park. The zoo will be closing in ten minutes. Please start making your way to the exit now." With a final pat of Rowan's fuzzy head, I left the enclosure and headed down the hall to the Wildlife Hospital.

"I'm really excited about this new show, but I'm going to miss Alessi," I said, looking down at my phone to see if my best friend had messaged me back. Her mom was one of the big cat caretakers and sometimes she came into work with her. We waved goodbye to some employees as we went to meet our parents in the visitors' center lobby. I looked up at my big brother, waiting for him to respond. He had recently dyed his black, wiry hair to a shocking blond that stood out against his dark skin and brown eyes.

My parents adopted Feye when I was just a baby. I've only ever known him as my big brother, even if we don't look alike. Our parents liked to joke that we were as thick as thieves, and called our adventures "Feye and Adrianna missions," because my mom was convinced we were on a mission to give her gray hairs. When we traveled along the Orinoco River in Venezuela, we brought piranhas into our tents to study how they ate, only to end up with bite marks and fishy-smelling blankets. During our last trip to Malaysia, we gave a group of orangutans all our bananas from our fruit stash. They made a terrible mess!

"I know you'll miss Alessi, but the *Wild Survival!* show has really taken off. We're going from a YouTube show to actual TV! Think of all the new animals we'll get to help here at the zoo. It's a good thing," Feye said, stretching his arms above his head and then ruffling my black hair. As I squirmed from his grip and ran through the visitors' center doors, I saw our dad motioning for us to hurry up.

Around here, Mom and Dad are famous. Well, as famous as wildlife conservationists can be. They had a popular YouTube channel called *Wild Survival!* where for years they showcased our family's travels around the world. We rescue animals from all over and then nurse them back to health at the zoo. The YouTube channel was originally just a way for them to share their passion for animals with a bigger audience, but lately we had gotten super popular. So popular that a television producer named Mr. Savage had recently reached out to my parents, asking if they wanted to do a television network show. My parents had jumped at the chance because a network show meant more money to fund animal rescues, and an opportunity to take our love of animals to a whole new audience.

I'd been begging our parents to let me help them with animal rescues on the YouTube channel, but they had a strict rule: "No on-screen until you turn thirteen." Something about keeping us safe and wanting to make sure we were mature enough to be in front of the camera. *Blah blah blah.* Feye got to be on camera and he made fart jokes at dinnertime—how mature is *that*?!

I had just recently turned twelve (*¡un año más!*) and my parents had given me the best news: that The Rule was about to go away because Mr. Savage said the television network wanted to involve the whole family in front of the cameras! There were still rules (of course! Sigh).

1. Safety first! If Mom and Dad thought a situation wasn't safe, Feye and I had to stop

what we were doing immediately and get out of harm's way.

2. I didn't do anything alone—ever. I always had to have an adult with me in the field.
3. The first two weeks would be a trial run. If I got into trouble, *poof!* I'd be back behind the scenes faster than you can say "Wild Survival!"

I couldn't wait to star in *Wild Survival!* with Feye and our parents. I knew they trusted me to be responsible because they let me do a lot of behind-the-scenes stuff, like give them ideas for segments to do on their show. I was proud that some of the video segments I had suggested were the ones with the highest views on our YouTube channel.

As Feye and I jogged up to our parents, Dad held out an iPad with pictures of a crocodile on it. "Mr. Savage sent over some info about an injured crocodile," Dad said. He swiped through some more pictures and started a short video. The camerawork was shaky, but we could see a large crocodile limp out of the water and into some thick forest greenery.

"That's the animal we are going to help out?" Feye asked, looking over Dad's shoulder. Feye had just turned fourteen and had grown taller than both our parents this summer. He took the iPad out of Dad's hands and swiped back to look at the photos.

Dad nodded, about to speak, when the lobby doors burst open and in walked a short man with piercing blue eyes.

"I can see it now. The debut episode of *Wild Survival!* filled with high action for two full hours. I can already picture the title: 'The Hunt for Cuba's Mega Croc.' And it's injured! Perfect! Full of dramatic boat shots through the mangroves as the clock ticks down to find this dangerous predator before it—" He paused at Dad's sudden intimidating look. Rick

MANGROVE TREE

- Worldwide, there are over eighty species of mangrove! Cuba is home to four different species: the red mangrove, the black mangrove, the white mangrove, and the button mangrove.
- Mangroves are the only kind of tree that can live in salt water.
- Mangrove trees' most distinctive feature is their tangle of roots that make them look as if they are climbing out of the water. These tall roots allow for the changes in tidal water levels throughout the day.

Savage was the producer of my parent's show. He had thinning red hair and a pale, freckled face. Mr. Savage wore the same look I'd always seen him in—aviator sunglasses, a blue button-up shirt, and white pants with crocodile-skin shoes (he swore they were fake). I wondered if he owned any other clothes.

Our parents had never done a network TV show before, let alone a production that was so flashy, but they'd put their trust in Mr. Savage to make a good series. Mr. Savage's brainstorms for the show usually involved the words "mega," "monster," "dangerous," or "man-eater" when describing animals. It made me roll my eyes, but I figured he knew what made TV shows sell.

"Where is this injured 'Mega Croc'?" our mom asked, taking the iPad from Feye to watch the video once more.

"Cuba," he said. "So we don't have a moment to lose. Locals say it was recently injured, and as you can tell, it needs immediate medical care. It probably can't move much, so it'll be easier to track down. I'll need you to pack up your things tonight so we can get out there quickly. We have a flight booked and ready!"

Tonight! I shivered with excitement. I couldn't wait to start our search for the injured crocodile!

CHAPTER TWO

I shifted uncomfortably in my seat as the airplane captain turned on the seat belt sign for landing.

"You nervous, A?" Feye asked, looking over at me from his *Aves de Cuba* field guide. He was obsessed with birds, but I could never understand the appeal. Sharks, tigers, and even crocodiles were far more interesting than chirpy birds. Feye already had his binoculars around his neck, ready to spot some new feathered friends. I rolled my eyes and looked out the window.

"A little. I just hope we can find the crocodile and get it safely back to the Wildlife Hospital. And not spend too much time on the extra dramatic stuff," I said, now able to see more of the island. Earlier during the flight, I'd overheard Mr. Savage talking to my parents about how the show would mostly focus on finding a legendary monster-sized crocodile in Cuba instead of the injured crocodile . . . how ridiculous!

"We all have the animal's safety in mind, even Mr. Savage," Feye said with confidence. I continued looking out the window, not wanting to think about Mr. Savage anymore. With a few bumps thanks to turbulence, we landed.

"How big do you think the crocodile is?" I asked Feye as I tried to get my luggage from the overhead compartment.

Feye shrugged, reached over, and grabbed my bag for me. "No idea. Maybe ten feet? Dad is better at guessing size than I am. But it definitely didn't seem big enough to be that 'Mega Croc' Mr. Savage keeps going on about."

Outside the plane, a big production bus was waiting for us. I saw Feye take his cell phone out, holding it up in the air while we walked toward the bus.

"No bars already! How am I going to let my fans know about our adventures?" He sighed.

I laughed. Feye considered himself an "influencer" on social media and liked to keep his fans up to date. I went ahead and checked my phone, too. I had only one fan—Alessi—but that was all I needed. But no bars for me either. Darn.

I climbed into the bus and took up a whole row as I got ready for the long ride ahead to the coast. I planned to study up on crocodiles with a book I'd brought with me, but before long I was fast asleep.

A jolt of the bus snapped me awake. I stretched and peered out the window. It was a blur of green as countryside whooshed by.

My mom poked her head up over the seat in

front of me. "Good, you're awake! We're almost there," she said before ducking back down.

Every time we rescue an animal, I always try to learn as much as I can about it. I cracked open my notebook and jotted down a few things I'd learned from my book before I drifted off.

Finally, the bus lurched to a stop and we all got off. I took my bags and handed them off to a crew member standing near a boat. This was how we were getting to our final destination: an archipelago, or chain of islands, in the southern part of Cuba. I looked outside at the mangroves hugging either side of the channel and remembered how Feye once said that they are hardy survivors. With their long webs of roots submerged in murky water, these beautiful trees thrive in conditions that would quickly kill most other plants. They really are true survivors—and home to such an incredible diversity of creatures.

THE AMERICAN CROCODILE

- Males can weigh over 1,000 pounds, females up to 400 pounds.
- Pretty shy creatures.
- Can lay up to 50 eggs at a time.
- *Biggest threats: loss of habitat and illegal killing.*

Night had fallen by the time our boat docked at a floating boat hotel. Our journey to come to the home of the injured crocodile had taken all day! We'd stay at the boat hotel for the next week as we tried to locate our croc.

As the adults got busy setting everything up, Feye and I went to our rooms to sleep for the rest of the night. I plopped down on the bed and looked around my room, realizing it didn't look that different from other hotels we had stayed in. If I didn't know any better, I wouldn't have known we were floating in the water!

The next morning, I woke up to the smell of my favorite breakfast—bacon and waffles! I shot out of bed and over to the window to soak in the orange-pink sunrise. From the second floor of the boat hotel, you could see for miles. It was then that it dawned on me how utterly alone we were. I couldn't even see another boat! The hotel was docked on the edge of a channel near a large cluster of trees. The water was so calm, it reflected the sunrise's rays like glass. From our main channel of water, many other smaller channels snaked in different directions, leading deeper into the dense forest. There were so many different paths to take and explore! I could hear the chittering of birds hidden in the mangroves' branches, almost like they were calling to me. I took a deep breath in, smiled, and headed downstairs to start the day.

"So, what's the plan for today?" Feye asked our parents, bits of bacon coming out of his full mouth as he spoke.

"Feye! *¿Donde están tus modales?* Manners, please!" our mom said. His face reddened as he mumbled sorry and wiped his mouth with a napkin.

Dad smiled. "Well, we're all going on a test run

of our equipment! We need to make sure our snorkeling gear works and doesn't have any leaks."

"I didn't pack any snorkel gear!" Feye and I said in unison, suddenly feeling very unprepared. How could we not have thought to bring our stuff?!

Mom laughed. "No, don't worry! We have new snorkel and dive gear that the network provided. It has the show's logo on it and everything so we can all match."

Mr. Savage opened the door, a cup of hot coffee in one hand (he lived on the stuff) and a big rolling bag in the other. "Here are the stars! Hope everyone slept well," he boomed.

He set his coffee cup down and lugged the big bag onto a chair. "Right, so outside we have all the gear you need to test this morning. Once you are done with breakfast, I want the family and their safety divers to get geared up in the scuba stuff first. Connor, as lead sound producer, you're in charge of making sure these fancy microphone face masks work."

Connor was our sound producer at Sacred Sanctuary and Zoological Park. He helped out with the YouTube show and set up the sound for our educational presentations at the zoo. Connor had been part of our team for what felt like forever. He and Feye were practically best friends because they both liked big cats and bird-watching.

"On it, boss," Connor said in his Australian accent. He, like Mr. Savage, also seemed to live on coffee . . . and banana bread. That was one of the reasons I liked him—he always had snacks in his pockets and he sometimes let me have some. Snacks like the last chocolate muffin he had on his plate.

Connor saw me eyeing it, let out a chuckle, and passed a chunk to me. "That's all you get, you dingus." I smiled and reached over to grab the butter to slather the muffin with.

As I shoved the muffin in my mouth, Feye grabbed my hand and said, "Connor, stop feeding her! We need to get ready!" He tugged me out of my chair and toward the gear Mr. Savage had put down nearby.

"Oi, I need to eat, too! Take your time," Connor said in between mouthfuls.

"Manners, Connor!" Feye teased, and stuck out his tongue.

"Feye! Stop sassing the poor guy and let him eat with the rest of the adults," our mother said, drinking her orange juice.

Feye had stopped listening as he rummaged through the bag with the new gear. He threw a wet suit and a bag at me without any warning, so I dropped both things. I grumbled as I picked up the stuff and headed upstairs after Feye to change. Not going to lie, we looked pretty darn professional in our new spiffy gear!

"Hey, kids!" we heard Connor yell from the boat docking station, on the other side of the kitchen. "Meet me by the boats for the trial dive!"

We didn't need to be told twice. We dashed toward his voice to meet up with him and the rest of the crew. Our parents were also in their wet suits now, sitting by the scuba tanks. As a crew member helped strap their tanks on, another busied themselves with tightening the full-face masks on us.

I have been scuba diving since I was ten years old and I have my Junior Open Water certification, but I had never worn a mask with a microphone before. It couldn't be that different, right? I started to take the microphone mask out of the bag it came in.

Connor plopped down next to me, smiling his big flashy smile, and said, "Not so fast, Adrianna. You've never put one of these on before, so I'm in charge of making sure you're comfortable with it."

He took the bag out of my hand and pulled out

a glossy black-and-blue mask that would cover my eyes and nose. Connor pointed to a button on the bottom right of the mask. "See this? That's the button you want to hit whenever you want to talk and have people hear you."

I nodded.

"You can't squeeze your nose like you would with a regular mask, so if you want to equalize your ears as you dive deeper so they don't hurt, you can push the mask up so it hits your nose," Connor explained. In scuba diving lingo, "equalizing" means to relieve the building pressure between the inside of your ears and the surrounding water. If you dive without equalizing your ears, it hurts really bad and you could damage your hearing!

I nodded again. "I'm a pro, Connor! Don't worry!"

He laughed. "I know, I know. Just remember to

breathe normally, okay? It might get a little sweaty in there around your mouth, but you should be fine."

I pulled the mask over and tugged at the straps to make it tight around my face. I gave everyone a thumbs-up and saw Mr. Savage walk toward us.

"All right, is everyone ready for a test dive?" Mr. Savage asked. We all gave the "okay" sign and he gave us one right back. "Whenever you're ready, just go to the bottom and meet your safety divers there. We'll run some sound tests to make sure we can hear you crystal clear up here and then you guys can come back up and test the snorkel gear."

Safety divers always dove with us to keep us safe in case of an emergency, like our air tanks springing a leak. They stayed close enough to help if anything went wrong, but far enough away to not be in the shot. Feye once said he wanted to be a safety diver when he grew up because they can also volunteer to be part of emergency, rescue, and investigative operations.

We gave one another kisses on the cheek—as we did before every adventure—and then looked at the water below. Our parents were the first to dive down, followed by Feye and then me. I released the air in my scuba vest, which was keeping me afloat at the surface, and let the weights in the vest take me under the water. As I began to sink under the surface, I felt water suddenly rush into my mask. That wasn't supposed to happen! My first instinct was to panic, but I quickly pushed those thoughts away and filled my scuba vest with air again to pop back up to the surface. I waved my arm frantically to signal something was wrong. Suddenly, I felt myself being yanked back to the dock.

"Are you okay?" Connor asked. "What happened?"

I tried to talk, but he shook his head and took the mask off.

"What did you say? I couldn't hear you through the mask."

"I don't know, it just started filling with water," I said. A crew member radioed down to my family to let them know I was experiencing technical difficulties but was fine.

Connor examined the mask to see if there was anything wrong, then looked back at me for a quick second before reaching both his hands behind his head and shaking loose his ponytail. He handed his hair tie to me and said, "It's your hair! Your long hair is getting in the way of the mask forming a proper seal around your face. Tie it up with this."

"Thanks, Connor!" I said as I pulled my hair back and made a quick braid. I looked at his shoulder-length hair and said, "Wow. Your hair is almost longer than mine!"

He handed me my mask back and winked. "You're just jealous of my beautiful locks!"

I coughed out a laugh and readjusted the mask back onto my face.

"All good?" Connor asked. I gave him the "okay" sign and jumped back into the water. This time when I dove down, no water came into the mask. I slowly sunk to the bottom, near the big metal structures that kept the boat hotel above the water.

"Can you hear me, Adrianna?" a crackly voice came through the mask. It sounded like Feye. He waved at me through the crystal clear teal water. I remembered to hit the button and replied, "Loud and clear!"

"Testing, testing, this is topside. Can you guys hear me?" I heard Connor say. One by one we let him know we could hear him perfectly. The next voice we heard over our headsets was Mr. Savage telling us to swim around the boat hotel to make sure our gear felt comfortable enough, and to stay alert for interesting wildlife.

"All right, Villalobos family, we want to show off Cuba's pristine marine habitat to the viewers. That means we're looking for beautiful coral, dramatic overhangs, colorful animals, big fish . . . and this place is ripe with sharks!" Mr. Savage said into our sound system. "I want Julio and Evelyn to talk about what they see, and kids, I want you to inject your enthusiasm into whatever they point out! We want excitement! Don't be afraid to play up being scared when a scary shark or monstrous eel comes out to play."

The habitat in front of us was far from scary. The coral reef, vibrant with life, was the healthiest I had seen while out diving. Small schools of colorful fish darted in unison between the coral that swayed gently with the current and bigger fish lazily eyeing them for a potential meal. I kept my eyes out for flamingo tongues, one of my favorite small animals in the western Atlantic Ocean.

It was like the coral reef was listening to my wishes because on a delicate sea fan was a cluster of flamingo tongues. I hit the microphone button and exclaimed, "Mom! Dad! Feye! Check out these beautiful flamingo tongues!"

I saw Mom turn around instantly and give me a thumbs-up. Flamingo tongues are a snail that eat away at soft coral, like the sea fan it rested on. I love their bright pink and orange colors and their cool black spots. The most fascinating thing about these snails is that this brightly colored part of them isn't their shell at all—it's actually the snail's soft tissue, which wraps around the entire shell!

As we swam to the front part of the hotel, near where we had first arrived, we could suddenly hear a lot of noise from the boat above. It sounded like running . . . Was something wrong?

"Hey, topside, this is Julio. Is everything okay? We hear a lot of noise above us," our dad asked.

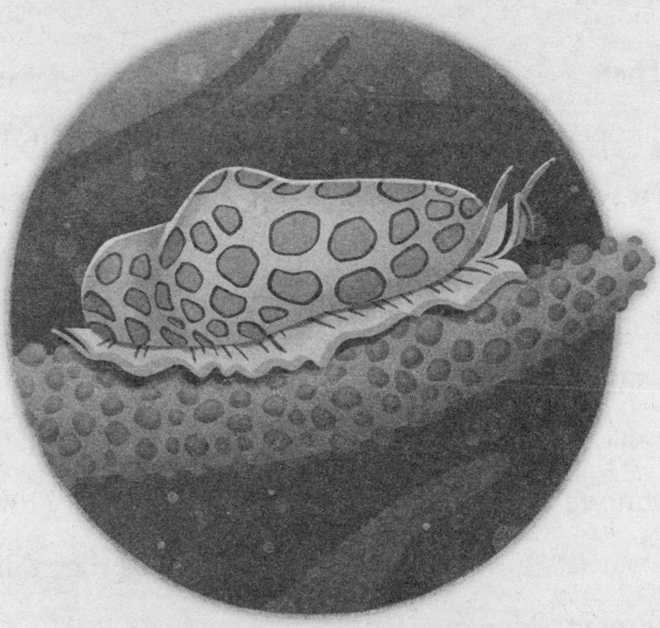

FLAMINGO TONGUE SNAIL

- The flamingo tongue's bright colors act as a warning to potential predators. Their coloring acts as a kind of STOP sign to say "Don't touch me! I'm poisonous!"
- These snails feast on soft species of coral like sea fans and whip corals.
- They prefer the warm waters of the Western Atlantic Ocean.

There was silence for a minute or two and we all stopped swimming, waiting for an answer. Our parents floated a bit closer to us, each holding one of our hands.

"Hey, guys, we have a big figure coming your way," Mr. Savage finally said over the radio. "We can't tell what it is and we're trying to identify it. Can you see it? It's just ahead of you!" The safety divers formed a protective circle around us as they talked through sign language.

The water visibility was a little bit murkier on this side of the hotel, but it wasn't impossible to see . . . Oh, there! Yes! I could see a big, slow-moving creature coming our way!

"It's a manatee!" our mom exclaimed. As the manatee got closer, we heard splashes above us and looked to see that we suddenly had two of the camera people with us. Mr. Savage must have asked them to join us to make sure their equipment worked, too.

We suddenly heard Mr. Savage over our headsets telling Mom to get closer to the manatee and talk about it.

She let go of Feye's hand and swam ahead, getting closer as she explained to the cameras what we were seeing. I struggled to pay attention to her as I looked at the big Antillean manatee. It had dark, round eyes and a wrinkly snout with whiskers. I'd never seen one up close and personal before!

As I saw Dad swim to meet Mom by the cameras and also narrate, I tried to remember what I had read about these manatees. They usually weren't more than twelve feet long, and this one looked smaller than that. It definitely didn't weigh as much as they usually could, which was up to 1,200 pounds.

"Very little is known about manatees in Cuba," I heard my dad say as the manatee went up to the surface to breathe.

"Kids, do you want to say anything? Get close to your parents so we can get you in the shot!" Mr. Savage said, and our safety divers led us to our mom and dad.

Feye hit his button before me. "Human threats to these gentle animals include them getting caught in fishing gear and hunting. It's illegal to hunt manatees, but some people still do."

"Perfect. Adrianna, anything to add? It seems the manatee is ready to swim off and we want one last shot of all of you with it before it does," said Mr. Savage.

This was my first big moment to speak on *Wild Survival!* I couldn't mess it up! But as I stared into the camera, I couldn't think of anything important to say.

"I'm sorry," I said, and Feye pointed to the side of his mask. Oh! I had forgotten to push the microphone button. I said sorry again, this time pushing the button, telling them I had nothing.

MANATEE

- Adult manatees can weigh up to 1,200 pounds!
- Manatees can spend up to half the day snacking on things like algae, sea grass, and mangrove leaves. Each day, an adult manatee can eat up to 10 percent of its body weight. For a 1,200 pound manatee, that's 120 pounds of food!
- Manatees are mammals, so they must come up to the water's surface. But they can hold their breath for up to twenty minutes!

"I think you need to study up on your Cuban wildlife, Adrianna," Mr. Savage said over our head-sets. "But at least we could hear you once you remembered to hit your microphone button. Great gear test run, Villalobos clan. Now, get back up here while I work with the camera crew down there."

I could feel my face heating up.

My family gave one another fist bumps as we made our way back up, but I couldn't help feeling disappointed that I couldn't even think of one measly manatee fact to share. I had to do better next time!

CHAPTER THREE

Our parents spent the morning shooting scenes with an overhead drone. Mr. Savage wanted to get a lot of shots of them looking dramatically over the side of the boat as they zipped around the mangroves. According to him, this scene would be the opening of the show and would introduce our parents as superhero wildlife defenders.

I had seen Dad practicing his best "dramatic serious hero" look in the mirror earlier, and I had burst out laughing so loudly he chased me from the room.

While they were out filming, Feye and I decided to stay behind with part of the crew to film some of the ecosystems around the floating boat hotel. Mark and Alice from the camera crew followed us around as we described the different animals we saw both under and above the water.

Nearby, deeper in the mangroves, was a small sandy spit where Cuban rock iguanas crawled around under the hot Caribbean sun. Mark and Alice suggested we stop to film them since we might not get another chance to have just us kids narrating. "All right, Feye, tell us a little bit about Cuba's reptiles and lead into talking about these iguanas. Adrianna, then we'll pan over to you and you can tell us more about them, okay?" Mark said once he had set up his camera to record us.

He hadn't noticed Feye leaning on a mangrove taking selfies. Mark frowned.

"Feye! Come on!" he said.

Feye held his hands up in defeat and stuffed his phone in his pocket.

"Hey, I need to remember my time here with pictures!" Feye said. "I go everywhere with this phone, so I don't forget a single moment."

He straightened his shirt and looked into the camera. "Cuba has over one hundred and thirty species of reptiles, and about eighty percent of them are endemic, meaning you can only find them here. Over half the reptiles are actually lizards, like the Cuban rock iguana!"

He continued, "The Cuban iguana can get up to five feet long and can weigh around fifteen pounds. These iguanas can be dark gray or brown, and they all have this beautiful banding around their bodies."

"Perfect! All right, let me watch this to make sure we've got a good shot," Mark said as his eyes focused on the camera screen, with Alice looking alongside him.

I pouted, feeling left out and thinking that my

CUBAN ROCK IGUANA

- Because Cuban rock iguanas can grow up to five feet long, they are one of the biggest lizards in the Caribbean.
- These lizards are primarily herbivores, meaning they eat mostly a plant-based diet. But they've also been known to eat things like crabs, fish, or birds.
- Cuban rock iguanas can live up to fifteen years.

brother was hogging all the camera time. I needed to prove I knew a lot, too! For instance, I knew that there were over eighty species of mangrove. Cuba was home to four of those: the red mangrove, the black mangrove, the white mangrove, and the button mangrove. I had seen their photos in books before, so I thought I would be pretty good at identifying them. I hadn't tried earlier, but since we were up close and personal now, I thought I could give it a shot. I stared at the mangrove in front of me and realized I had no idea which one it was!

With a shrug, I gave up and instead joined Feye in watching the yellow-brown, scaly iguanas up above in the mangrove branches. Most were sleeping, their beady red eyes hidden. One stirred, and I pointed it out to Feye so he could see the large lizard begin to climb up a branch. The thick tail of the iguana swung from side to side and its claws made a *scratch* noise against the mangrove wood.

"If we're lucky, we might see—" Feye stopped short as the climbing iguana launched itself from the branch above into the water below.

"Whoa!" I cried. We both scrambled closer to watch the iguana swim easily in the murky green-gray water.

Mark and Alice were still hunched over the camera screen, talking about something in hushed tones. They had completely missed the amazing iguana action!

"What a spot!" Mark said, finally looking up. "We already have a lot of great footage, and we're just getting started. Now we just need to find this Mega Croc Savage keeps going on about."

"I thought Mr. Savage just wanted 'Mega Croc' in the title of the show to attract viewers," I said.

"The injured croc is big, but I don't know if I'd call it 'mega,'" Feye added.

Alice shook her head. "There's a legend around

here that there's a monster croc. It's supposed to be like twenty-five feet long, weigh a few tons, and be an absolute terror."

"But . . . it's legendary. So, it couldn't really exist, surely," Feye said slowly.

Feye and I were about to ask more questions, but we heard the roar of a boat engine and turned to see our parents and Mr. Savage heading our way.

"Time for lunch!" my mom called. "I can't wait to hear about what you saw this morning!"

As we sat down for lunch, I shot a glance over at my brother, and then to Mr. Savage. I wiggled my eyebrows in the universal signal for "Should I ask him about the Mega Croc?" Feye nodded slightly.

"Hey, Mr. Savage?" I started.

He looked up at me, wiping his mouth with a napkin. "Yes, Adrianna?" he asked.

"Can you tell us more about this Mega Croc?"

I could tell my dad wanted to interject because his mouth opened up, but it quickly shut when Mr. Savage waved at him and chuckled. "Of course I can!" He began to tell us how the locals have been talking about a massive crocodile that could be a hybrid between the American crocodile, like the injured one we were looking for, and the Cuban crocodile.

"It isn't totally out of the question," our dad hesitantly told Mr. Savage when he was done with his tale. "The Cuban crocodiles are losing their genetic identity because they're interbreeding with the more abundant cousin, the American crocodile."

We had heard about Cuban crocodiles before. Some family friends had seen them in the wild before and were terrified—one said it was like looking at a devil because of their raised eyebrow ridges and dark eyes.

"The Cuban crocodiles could once be found

roaming all throughout Cuba but are now only found in large numbers in the Zapata Swamp," my mom added.

"The cameras aren't rolling, you know," Feye joked. Mom stuck her tongue out and we all laughed.

"Now you've said it yourself! The genes of two dangerous predators mixed into one super-aggressive crocodile," Mr. Savage exclaimed, his drink slamming down onto the table for emphasis as he talked. "Maybe the injured crocodile got into a tussle with the Mega Croc!"

I could see my mom frowning.

"Do you think the injured croc has died?" asked Feye.

"No, I don't think it did. It may be hiding, though. Lying low," said our dad.

Suddenly, all our radios crackled to life as someone said, "*¿Están ustedes allí?* Are you guys there? We have a crocodile sighting! *¡Vemos un cocodrilo!*"

Our mother grabbed the nearest radio. "We're here. Where is it?"

"It's near your boat hotel! And it is HUGE!!" the voice said.

I gasped. Could this be one of the crocodiles we were looking for?

CHAPTER FOUR

Everyone sat frozen until Mr. Savage started barking orders. "All right! Julio, grab the tracking gear. Evelyn, get the medical kit just in case this croc is the injured one we've been searching for. Kids, why don't you come along for this, too."

"Yes!" I cried. Immediately, Feye and I clambered onto the boat before Mr. Savage could change his mind. My parents took off in different directions to gather supplies. While they packed our boat, another set of crew members went ahead to see if they could find and wrangle the crocodile.

In just a few minutes, our second boat was ready

to go, and we were speeding through the ocean. The curved white roots of the mangrove trees rose out of the blue-green water. Overhead, their leafy branches formed a vivid green tunnel of sorts.

As we rounded a bend and came into a more open section of the channel, we easily spotted the first team's bright white boat against the dull brackish water.

Our boat slowed to a stop, and Mr. Savage got on the radio. "What's happening, Pablo?" he asked the other boat's captain.

"It's a big croc all right!" Pablo's gravelly voice said over the radio. "But it isn't the injured one. The *muchachos* lured it out of the water with some chicken and have it tied up for you."

Our boat slowly motored forward to join the other and Pablo waved us over. Behind him, on a small stretch of muddy land, a large croc had been restrained by his crew.

"Aw, man. I really wanted to see them pull the croc out of the water," Feye said.

"Well, we're just getting started, Feye!" my mom said. "We promised some of our Cuban university friends that we'd put tags on any crocs we found. The information the tags collect will help them figure out how these large predators use their habitat."

Mr. Savage stroked his chin, a glint in his eye. "Footage of you all tagging a croc is less exciting than footage of the guys wrestling one, but we'll make it work!" He grinned like he'd made a very funny joke, but I could see my parents exchange an exasperated look behind his back.

My mother started poking around the boxes of gear, pulling out the tagging equipment.

"Can we help?" I asked, dying to be a part of the action—*finally*.

"Can they, Julio?" Mr. Savage asked our dad. I

could see him perk up at the prospect of getting us all on camera at the same time.

"Feye has put tags on smaller crocs before. Not much different to put a tag on a larger croc!" Dad said, shrugging.

"And what about me?" I asked, not wanting to be left out.

They all turned to me. Dad looked concerned, but Mom took my hand and smiled. "I've got a very special job for you," she said.

"Fantastic!" Mr. Savage cheered. "The croc is already prepped, so let's tag this bad boy up and inject some science into our episode!"

My mom quickly set out the tracker and a small pot of glue on a tray and handed it to me. "Here's your very important job," she said. "Prepping the tracking device for Feye!" She grinned triumphantly.

All I had to do was add enough glue to the tag to make sure it really stuck on the croc. While it wasn't the most exciting job, I got to participate, which was something! I'd done this many times before at home but never with cameras watching me.

Radio tracking is a great way to keep tabs on an animal. The tags aren't very big, so they don't bother the crocodile, but they emit a powerful signal that allows us to see where they go. For animals like crocodiles, the best place to put the small transmitter is on their back, right where their head ends and their body begins.

I quickly undid the top of the glue and grabbed a brush.

"Remember, Adrianna, just enough to make it stick—too much or too little, and it could fall off," my mom said before hopping out of the boat to go consult with Mr. Savage.

"I know, I know," I muttered to myself. Carefully, I applied a layer of glue at the bottom of the tracking device. The last thing I wanted was for this tag to come loose! It was a prime opportunity for us to find other crocodiles—maybe even the Mega Croc we'd heard so much about! I decided to put some glue on the sides of the tracking device, too, just in case.

I heard a squelching noise and saw Feye make his way through the mud toward the side of the boat.

"They're ready for the tag, Adrianna," he said, holding out his hand.

I couldn't believe how lucky Feye was, getting to place the first tracker of our adventure! Behind him, our family and some of the crew were busy taking measurements and some blood and tissue samples from the crocodile. I saw them try to angle the crocodile into perfect release position. As soon as the tracker was on the croc, they'd want to get it back into the water and on its way. I quickly put a tiny bit more glue on the sides and bottom of the tag and gently handed it over to Feye.

He grabbed the tag and walked back to our

parents. My dad stood at the croc's massive shoulder, so he could help direct Feye. I sealed up the glue and hopped over the boat's side to join my family. I didn't want to miss seeing the huge animal swim back into the water.

The mouth of the big croc was held shut by rope and its eyes were covered with a damp cloth to help keep it calm. Crew members gripped the croc all along its scaly body to hold it still so Feye could safely put the tag on its back.

He leaned forward carefully, placed the tracker, and then started to stand. But suddenly, Feye let out a yelp. "Dad, I'm stuck!" he cried in a slightly panicked voice.

My stomach dropped. He had just put all his body weight on top of the tag to make sure it really stuck to the crocodile—and now his hand was also attached!

Feye tugged at his hand, cursing under his breath.

Dad signaled for another crew member to come take over his position at the crocodile's shoulder. "Now, don't panic, Feye," Dad said. "Keep breathing. It's important to stay calm. I'm going to take a look now. Just keep breathing and listening to the sound of my voice."

I realized then that I had also stopped breathing. I gulped in a big lungful of air and watched as my dad changed positions with the crew member who was coming to take over at the shoulder. But as the new crew member swapped in, he moved too quickly, and the damp towel that had been covering the crocodile's eyes suddenly slipped off.

Now able to see, the croc began to jerk from side to side, trying to get free.

The crew members hadn't been expecting that, and some lost their grips on the big animal. With a crack of its tail, the crocodile was able to inch closer toward the water—with my brother's hand still stuck to it.

"Dad!" Feye yelled, any brief calmness now completely erased.

Out of the corner of my eye, I saw Connor and the rest of the sound crew throw their boom microphones down and run over to jump on top of the massive crocodile. Someone tried to readjust the towel back over the croc's eyes, but in the confusion I couldn't tell who it was.

"We can't hold him much longer!" a voice called as the crocodile once more squirmed closer to the water. *This can't be happening . . . this can't be happening . . .* I hadn't realized I had taken a few steps back until my head hit the side of the boat.

"Feye, this is going to hurt, sorry!" I heard my dad say, as he tugged at Feye's hand.

Both of them jerked backward. Feye's hand was

finally free. Feye cried out and my mom swooped in to drag him away from the crocodile.

"He's loose! Let the big croc go! NOW!" Mr. Savage yelled. The team leapt off the crocodile and the enormous animal lurched forward and disappeared into the murky water.

CHAPTER FIVE

I couldn't move. *What had just happened?!*

I looked at my brother, who was in our mother's arms, holding his hand close to his chest as she kissed his forehead. Our set medic, Miguel, rushed past me with his kit.

"Let's all give them some room," Mr. Savage called, motioning people away from where they had started to congregate around Feye and my mom.

Now that the tense moment was over, the crew began to clean up. Everyone was covered in mud from struggling with the crocodile. My stomach did flip-flops. Shakily, I made my way across the bank toward my brother. I was the one who had prepared the tracker. Had I messed something up? Or had Feye put it on the wrong way?

"Adrianna!" Suddenly, my dad loomed in front of me, his mouth pressed into a hard line. "Just how much glue did you put on that tracking device?" His tone was measured, but I could tell from the pulsing vein in his forehead that he was trying very hard not to yell.

Oh no. "Not that much," I said in a small voice. But I couldn't lie. "Just some on the bottom . . . and a tiny bit on the sides," I finished, looking down at my mud-caked boots.

"Oh, Adrianna!" My dad took a deep breath. "What were you thinking? That's not how we taught you to prepare them."

"I'm sorry," I squeaked. "I just really didn't want it to fall off. I didn't think—"

"You didn't think! That's exactly the problem.

Your brother could have been really hurt, Adrianna. When we're out here filming, you have to follow our instructions at all times. I know this is all new and exciting, but you can't get caught up and forget the basics." My dad gestured around at the filming crew packing up their equipment.

My cheeks burned. I couldn't believe my dad thought I was so distracted by a couple of extra cameras that I couldn't handle a simple gluing task.

Before I could respond, Mom and Feye made their way to us. Feye clutched his hand, two fingers swathed in gauze.

"Feye, I'm so, so sorry," I said. But he didn't say anything. He just walked past me and went to sit on the boat, cradling his injured hand in his lap.

"What happened?" Mom asked, her full attention now on me and my dad.

Tears started to sting the back of my eyes. "I put too much glue on the tracking device. I know you always say not to do too much, but I thought adding some to the sides would make sure it stayed on . . ." I trailed off as I saw the disappointment on my mom's face. *"Lo siento mucho."*

"I know that you're sorry," my dad said. "But we can't ignore the fact that this was a big mistake." He and my mom shared a long look before he continued. "We wanted to give you a chance to be on camera with us. But it's clear you're not quite ready."

I gasped. "No! I am ready! I just—"

My mom raised her hand to cut me off. "This isn't a forever ban. We'll just have to see how it goes. But you're grounded for now."

I opened my mouth to say something, but my throat felt drier than a desert. I closed it back up and felt tears start to slide down my cheeks.

The ride back to the floating boat hotel was quieter than usual. The only noise came from the boat engine, the bugs chirping as the sun set behind the mangrove forest, and my occasional sniffle.

It was a mistake! One I certainly wouldn't be making again. And what made it worse was that Feye didn't even want to hear my apology. Once we docked back at the boat hotel that was serving as our base camp, he pushed past me without a word and stomped inside.

My mom shrugged. "He needs a little time, Adrianna," she said softly. I nodded but still hurried after Feye to try to explain. I caught up to him just as he was heading into his bunk room.

"I'm so sorry, Feye," I said. "I can't say it enough. I didn't mean to put you in danger."

"But you did." He said it flatly, his nostrils flaring.

"Not on purpose! You know that!" I said.

"Look, my hand hurts, and I'm tired. I'm heading to bed." He turned away from me.

"I love you, bro," I said, tears blurring my vision.

Feye paused. I saw his shoulders relax just a little bit. "I know, Adrianna. I love you, too."

With that he walked away, disappearing into his room. I sniffed one last time and rubbed my eyes clear of any remaining tears. I felt terrible, but what I needed now was a way to prove to everyone that I did know what I was doing. That I could be trusted. If I could do that, maybe Feye would forgive me. And my parents would let me back on the show. I made my way toward the boat hotel bathrooms but stopped when I heard voices coming from my parents' room.

"Listen, I understand, but the network wants the whole family in the show. Adrianna is part of the big-picture vision for the series," I heard Mr. Savage say to my parents.

I peeked around the doorframe for a second to see my dad's frowning face. I ducked back before anyone could spot me.

"Today was not a good start to things, Rick," my dad said. "Adrianna's just not ready. Family comes first."

"Of course, of course. Well, if I can't change your mind . . ." Mr. Savage trailed off hopefully.

"Thanks for understanding, Rick," my mom said.

I heard rustling noises as the grown-ups stood. I darted back down the hall to my room. The last thing I needed was to get caught eavesdropping!

So that was it . . . I was off the show.

Well, not if I had anything to say about it.

CHAPTER SIX

As I sat down at the table for breakfast, Connor gave me a small, reassuring smile. At least one person wasn't mad at me. I was slathering my toast in butter when Mr. Savage walked in with a stack of papers.

"We are changing tactics today after yesterday's accident!" he said. "We want the whole family involved, so we're moving our visit to the nearby crocodile breeding farm up a few days. I'd like us all to learn more about these Cuban crocodiles." Mr. Savage looked at my parents. "Is it okay if we bring Adrianna along? No filming of the kids; this is all educational."

My parents, food in both their mouths, looked at each other. Dad was the first to swallow and speak. "So long as she gets no camera time, yes. We are firm on no filming."

Mr. Savage clapped his hands. "Perfect! Wheels up in thirty minutes, so read these as you eat!" he said, tossing some pamphlets on the breakfast table. As quickly as he came in, he left.

I bit into my now-buttered toast, crinkling my nose as Connor spread the Vegemite he always brought with him onto his own. I was fully engrossed in the pamphlet when I felt a stern hand on my shoulder. I looked up to see my dad, asking if I was ready to go.

"This is a field trip, so you can come, but no camera time," he reiterated. I nodded, keeping my head down, and we all headed to the boat.

I climbed in and sat toward the front of the boat. I closed my eyes as the boat picked up speed, happy to focus on the wind and the occasional wave splashing me. It wasn't long before the boat captain slowly made his way to the port. I spotted two big vans and a small group of people waving at us. I smiled and waved back.

"*¡Hola familia Villalobos!*" the man in front of the group called.

Our boat hit the dock with a gentle thud, and my dad tossed one of the lines to secure the boat up to the leader, who took it and expertly knotted us in place. My dad reached up to clasp the man's hand in a handshake and brought him into a hug.

"Soriano, it's been a while! How are you, *mi amigo*?" Dad said, a big smile on his face.

"Good, especially now that you are all here! Will these be enough to take you to the farm?" Soriano said, pointing to the vans waiting for us.

"They will do just fine," Mr. Savage said. "Rick

Savage, nice to meet you, Soriano. Thank you for hosting us."

"Ah, anything for Julio here. And this must be your *familia*!"

We all climbed out and shook Soriano's hand. I made sure to give him a big smile and a firm handshake. I wanted to make a good impression and prove to my parents that I could be mature and responsible. I *had* to get back on the show!

As the vans pulled into the crocodile farm, we passed a big wooden sign that said BIENVENIDOS. A few baby crocodiles lounged near a lake behind the fence. They paid no attention to us as the vans drove by and parked near the entrance of a plain brick building.

We piled out of the vans, and Soriano led us back to an open-air pen. It held what looked to be hundreds of black-and-yellow Cuban crocodiles, napping under the hot Caribbean sun.

"Welcome to one of the oldest Cuban crocodile breeding farms here in Zapata. Here we breed the critically endangered Cuban crocodile in Zapata Swamp, Cuba's largest wetland. We have over two thousand individual crocodiles, but it's estimated that there are very few left in the wild," Soriano explained.

I couldn't help but get lost in the eyes of the nearest crocodile. It was not much bigger than my two hands put together. Its pale snout was covered in dark spots, and its yellow-green eyes looked as if they were sizing me up.

"Adrianna! Keep up!" Dad called out to me, breaking the spell.

We all walked around the pen and into the building itself. Lining the walls of the hallway were WANTED posters with different mug shots.

CUBAN CROCODILE

- Cuban crocodiles are very good swimmers and are also great at both walking and leaping. Agile both on land and in the water, they've even been known to leap out of the water to catch birds!
- Like many reptiles, Cuban crocodiles cannot generate body heat on their own. They gravitate toward sunny spots in the morning to help raise their body temperature.
- They have the smallest range of any crocodile–currently just 200 square miles in two different regions in Cuba: Zapata Swamp and Lanier Swamp.

I was surprised to see the sea of faces with grim headlines underneath each one:

WANTED FOR POACHING

WANTED FOR ILLEGAL WILDLIFE TRAFFICKING

WANTED FOR ILLEGAL WILDLIFE TRADING

The list went on and on. All the people looked mean. I saw Feye out of the corner of my eye taking photos with his phone. *More content for his Instagram when we finally get service again.* I rolled my eyes.

"What are all of these?" I asked Soriano, gesturing at the posters.

"One of the biggest problems facing our crocodiles these days is overhunting," Soriano explained. "A lot of the poachers here are a big problem for the conservation work we do."

"What are the crocs hunted for?" Mr. Savage asked, looking closely at some of the WANTED posters.

"Well, their skin is used for a variety of things such as purses, belts, boots, wallets, and briefcases.

Some people want crocodile heads to mount on their walls; some want their teeth for necklaces. Their meat is sold as a delicacy—and their eggs fetch a pretty penny, too," Soriano explained.

We passed a big green door that had a WANTED poster with a man and a woman snarling in their pictures. I quickly tore my eyes from their gaze and hurried to catch up with our group.

It was then that I noticed that Mr. Savage had also seen the poster and stopped, staring hard at the image of the man and woman on the door.

Soriano saw this and made his way back to Mr. Savage and the posters, the rest of us following him. He pointed to the words under their pictures. ARMED AND EXTREMELY DANGEROUS was written in bold red letters.

"Aren't all poachers armed and extremely dangerous?" Feye asked.

Soriano shook his head. "Not like these two.

They're clever and are okay with hurting people to get the animal they're after. The local authorities have been tracking them for the past few weeks with no good leads. Watch out for them, okay?" he warned. With one more glare at the poster, he led our group down the hallway. Mr. Savage kept looking back at the poster.

"Do you think the Mega Croc might have been hunted for its hide?" I wondered out loud.

Before Mr. Savage could say anything, I heard Soriano laugh. "Mega Croc? Are you guys looking for that legend as well?" He shook his head.

"Well, we're looking for a big, injured crocodile," Dad clarified.

"You've heard of the Mega Croc?" Feye asked.

"It's just a story," Soriano said. "People think there is this giant crocodile that has gone around terrorizing coastal communities and lives somewhere in Zapata. Some want to kill it out of fear, some want to kill it for its hide. A big croc hide sells for a lot of money if you know the right buyers."

"Have you seen any big crocodiles lately?" Mr. Savage asked Soriano.

"A few, but nothing like the legendary Mega Croc. You guys aren't the only ones looking for big crocs; poachers are around, too, especially those two who I just showed you. They've already hurt a lot of crocodiles and people in their quest to find this Mega Croc. So be careful," Soriano warned again. We all nodded, understanding the caution in his voice.

I turned to Feye and whispered, "Do you think the injured crocodile crossed paths with the poachers and that's why it got hurt?"

He just shrugged his shoulders. He still wasn't talking to me.

"But enough about urban legends. Let me show you some cool *real* crocs!" Soriano said, motioning us to follow him outside.

CHAPTER SEVEN

"Thank you for a wonderful tour of the farm, Soriano! We really appreciate it and got some great up-close footage of the crocs," Mr. Savage said enthusiastically, pumping Soriano's hand up and down in a handshake.

"You're welcome. Thank you for coming!" Soriano waved at us as we climbed into the vans.

"All right, guys, we are going to stick around Zapata for the rest of the day to see if we can spot some more of these Cuban crocodiles. We won't film the kids, we just want some good nature shots," said Mr. Savage.

Mom and Dad nodded in agreement.

"I reserved us a spot in a nearby site close to the water where we can set up for lunch, and then we'll divide and conquer to find some crocs! Raoul, rev up this van and get us out of here," Mr. Savage said.

Soon we were bumping down the dirt roads toward the new site. The first thing I noticed when we arrived was that it had netting around its entire perimeter.

"What is this net for?" I asked as we climbed out.

"It's to keep the Cuban crocs out. It's not always successful, though," Feye answered. *He speaks!* I cheered internally. It was the first time he had spoken to me the whole day. I handed him a sandwich from our backpack. He reached out with his bandaged hand and took it gently.

Feye and I munched on our ham-and-cheese sandwiches, alternating each bite with a salted potato chip. Our parents ate quickly and prepped to go out croc spotting with a camera crew.

"Feye, watch after your sister!" my mom called before climbing into one of the boats.

We both rolled our eyes and even shared a smile. Progress.

One of the smaller boats was pushed up onto the sand, back by a hammock that was tied between two trees near the water. It didn't take long for Connor to hop into the hammock, full from his lunch and ready for a nap. Our parents were helping load the drone onto their boat and waved at us.

"Be back in twenty minutes, please!" Mr. Savage said in between mouthfuls.

"You got it, boss!" Alice yelled as Mark expertly maneuvered the boat out of the sand and into the mangrove channel.

I grabbed the nearby cooler to see if we had any cold drinks and instead saw raw frozen chicken wings in plastic wrap. "Ew! Mr. Savage, what is chicken doing in the cooler?" I asked, putting the top back on the cooler.

"It's for dinner! Don't touch it," he said, looking down at his phone and hardly paying attention to me.

"A, you looking for water? I've got some," Feye said, now sitting inside the van and waving a small fan in front of his sweaty face. I took the drink from his hand, took a sip, and handed it back.

"Thanks."

"No problem. But sit outside the van. It's already hot enough here," he said. He was also distracted, reading his bird book.

I looked around for a spot to sit and wandered toward Connor. I noticed that the protective netting was missing a section near Connor's hammock. The old and tattered chunk of netting lay nearby on the sand.

"Not much good that'll do . . ." I mumbled. A slight breeze coursed through the campsite and it felt good on my hot skin. Maybe I could make myself useful and put the netting back up.

I tiptoed over the crunchy leaves, trying to come up with a plan to fix the net. I wasn't staring at the water for too long when what looked like a log suddenly popped up from the depths. I waited for it to float down the channel like the leaves had.

Except it didn't.

It stayed perfectly still.

And then it blinked at me.

I took a step back. That was no log swimming through the water and heading right toward our sleeping sound producer.

"CONNOR!" I yelled, my hands cupped around my mouth. "Connor! Wake up! There's a crocodile coming your way!"

Connor raised his head to look at me, then he turned to see the crocodile.

Feye and Mr. Savage ran over to me. We stood

back and watched in horror as the crocodile slowly heaved itself out of the water.

"What do we do?" Feye asked, his eyes bulging in shock.

Think, Adrianna! Think! my inner voice said. *What can you use to distract the croc?*

Food, crocodiles could be distracted by food.

What did crocs eat?

Did we even *have* any food?

"The chicken!" I shouted. I darted over to the nearby cooler and grabbed some of the frozen raw chicken wings. I ran back over to Mr. Savage. "Distract the crocodile with this!" I said.

"Me?!" Mr. Savage said, eyes darting between the chicken I held in my hands and the crocodile. But he only hesitated for a moment before quickly jogging to the other side of the channel. "Hey! Hey, crocodile! Look what I have!" he yelled, looking directly at the crocodile and waving his arms.

The crocodile stopped walking and looked at Mr. Savage with interest. Mr. Savage dropped the chicken at his feet and raised one wing into the air. “See this? It’s food! Come here!” he yelled, waving the chicken and then throwing it into the channel. The crocodile stared at where the chicken splashed, still unmoving.

“Come on, don’t waste it! Get the chicken!” Mr. Savage yelled again, picking up another piece and throwing it in.

The crocodile suddenly lurched toward Mr. Savage, and I realized that I hadn’t thought this far ahead in my plan . . .

CHAPTER EIGHT

On land, crocodiles aren't all that fast. They rely on their sneakiness to launch surprise attacks. But when one is headed right toward you, it seems like they're faster than a race car!

The crocodile was coming right for Mr. Savage. I thought about telling him to scramble up a nearby tree, but the croc suddenly turned to go back into the water. Mr. Savage threw the last two pieces of chicken into the water and then sprinted back toward the van quicker than I had ever seen him move.

Connor finally hauled himself out of the

hammock and came to join us at the van. "Wow," he said. "No more sleeping by the water's edge, I think!"

We all shared a shaky laugh.

Feye opened his mouth to say something, but the roar of a boat engine interrupted us. Turning to the mangrove channel, we saw my parents' boat pull up. They were waving frantically at us.

"It's probably better if I tell them about this incident," Mr. Savage said. I was not going to argue with him. "You kids wait here."

My parents quickly got out of the boat as it docked, yelling, "Are you all okay?! We just saw what happened on the drone!"

I watched my parents talk to Mr. Savage. Suddenly, I heard my mother say, "Adrianna did what?" Yikes. I hoped she wasn't mad that the whole chicken thing had been my idea.

Connor and Mr. Savage were both speaking now, their animated hand gestures giving me only small clues as to what was happening. Mom held up both her hands to stop them from talking. She said something and pointed to the van, and both Connor and Mr. Savage nodded.

"Adrianna Villalobos!" my mother called as she stomped over to me. My dad and Connor followed close behind.

"Hi, Mom," I said, my voice barely above a whisper. If crocodiles could survive near extinction, I could survive my mom being mad at me . . . right?

"Connor and Mr. Savage told us you did some quick thinking with giving Mr. Savage the chicken to distract the crocodile. That was pretty . . . impressive."

I breathed a sigh of relief.

"She really saved my butt back there, Evelyn," Connor said. "She knows a lot about these animals and their instincts. It's almost like she should have her own TV show . . ."

I silently mouthed "*gracias*" to Connor and he winked at me.

My parents both sighed.

"We're definitely proud of you, *mi nena,*" Dad said.

I threw myself at them, giving them a big hug. "Proud enough to put me back on camera?" I asked, hopeful.

My mom frowned. "I don't know . . ."

"Well, what about a teeny, tiny on-camera field trip with us?" Mark the cameraman suggested.

"What?" Mom asked.

"Connor and I are filming a mini assignment about the working dogs of Cuba. Why don't we bring Adrianna along, and she can be the face of that segment?" Mark said.

"She'll be safe. No crocs there!" Connor smiled, flashing a thumbs-up sign.

Mom's stern expression softened, and she laughed.

After my parents looked at each other for what felt like an eternity, Mom finally relented. "Fine. She can go."

I let out a cheer and shared a fist bump with Connor and Mark. "Let's go!" I cried. "Before she changes her mind!"

CHAPTER NINE

The cobbled streets of the small Cuban town were just as full of dogs as they were of people. While some dogs had collars, most of them were skinny strays.

"All right, Adrianna. Just like we practiced, talk about the dogs of Cuba for a little bit," Mark said.

I nodded and looked at the camera, its red light now on to signal that Mark was rolling. I was surrounded by dogs here in Cuba, most of them *satos*, or mutts, that often go unnoticed. As we walked along these colorful streets, I couldn't help but pay attention to every single puppy.

"Look at that one over there! His fluffy ears are so cute!" I yelled.

I was pretty sure the guys already regretted bringing me along for this segment. But it wasn't my fault the dogs had all completely stolen my heart!

I bent down and held out a dog treat to a small, fluffy white dog passing by. "Check it out! It's a bichon," I said. I once wanted a bichon because they reminded me of clouds, and I was surprised to see one as a stray here. She wagged her tail and trotted toward me. Her cold snout pressed up against my hand as she lapped up the dog treat and looked for more.

It wasn't until she shook her whole body that I heard the familiar jingle of a collar. Hidden under her fluffy fur was a small ID badge clipped on her collar. I showed it off to the camera. "Throughout the country, dogs are hired for very important jobs! They are given official ID badges like this one, a place to live, and medical care from local vets. Some dogs even hang out with the police and help fight crime."

The puppy nuzzled up to me as I let go of her collar and took another dog treat out of the plastic baggie I had in my pocket. I smiled back at the camera as she began gleefully barking for more treats.

"Cut! Perfect, Adrianna. Why don't you take a quick break while I fiddle around with the settings?" Mark said, now tweaking buttons and knobs on his camera.

I sat down and leaned against the bright pink storefront we had been filming in front of. Although my bag of treats was hidden safely away in my pocket, the bichon was still wagging her tail hoping I would feed her more. It attracted the attention of more stray dogs, who came over and started sniffing me.

The dogs were of all sizes—some looked like big German shepherds and some looked like teeny, tiny Chihuahuas. Their wet noses and whiskers tickled me as they smelled me all over. I laughed, pushing some of them away, showing them my hands were empty. When they realized I didn't have any more food, their attention turned elsewhere. I put my head down on my knees, letting the cool breeze dry some of the sweat on my neck. I admired a pretty little hummingbird hovering by a potted flowering plant. It looked like an Elfin bee hummingbird! They were the smallest hummingbirds in the world. But before I could get my phone out to snap a picture, the sound of voices speaking in English distracted me.

"This is a disaster! If we don't find this monster soon, we're in deep trouble," said a deep, gruff voice in a thick Irish accent. A couple dressed in khaki were close enough that I could hear their conversation.

ELFIN BEE HUMMINGBIRD

- This tiny hummingbird is completely unique to Cuba–it doesn't live anywhere else.
- It weighs less than a single dime and is only two inches long from beak to tail.
- Unsurprisingly, this mini bird lays very mini eggs–each is only about the size of a pea!

The man had the beginning of a beard, sort of like my dad when he doesn't shave for a whole week.

The stranger took off his sunglasses to read his phone, and I felt a jolt of recognition. The man in front of me was the same man from the WANTED poster we had seen at the crocodile center! My mouth fell open. Soriano had warned us that this man and his partner were particularly dangerous. I sat frozen, unsure what to do.

I sneaked a glance at the pale woman next to the man with the sunglasses. They sure didn't look that dangerous. Or armed. They kind of just looked like tourists who were mad their vacation wasn't going as planned. Slowly, I pulled out my cell phone. If I could angle this right, I might be able to snap a photo.

Suddenly, I felt a cold snout push my knee a few times, demanding attention. I looked down to meet warm brown eyes and a face that was a mixture of gold, black, and white. The dog almost looked like he was smiling, and his tail wagged back and forth. I thought he must be looking for food, but his small, black-and-gray body wasn't as skinny as the other stray dogs.

"Hey, buddy. Are you lost?" I asked, looking for a collar. I held my hand out for him to sniff, which he did, and then he began licking my fingers. He must have been tasting the remnants of the bacon treat I had just given the other puppy!

I scratched behind his ear and smiled as his tail continued to wag. He let out a happy bark. "What a good boy you are!" I whispered, continuing to scratch. By the time I looked back up, the poachers had disappeared. Darn it! I had missed my chance.

"I see you've made a friend!" Mark laughed, looking up from his camera and giving me a wink.

"It seems so!" I grinned back. "Hey, Mark, I think I just saw—"

"We're late!" Mark cried, glancing down at his watch. "Time for the next shot! Let's get a move on, everyone."

I stood up, sighing. I would have to tell them about the poachers later. I hoped that they weren't as dangerous as Soriano had made them out to be . . .

CHAPTER TEN

We spent the afternoon shooting scenes in three different locations with all sorts of dogs. Throughout it all, the small black-and-gray dog we had met at the store followed us around. He seemed especially fond of Connor and kept going back to him for extra pets.

"Come on, Duke," I yelled. The dog gave a happy bark and came running over from the light post he had been sniffing.

"Adrianna, you gave the dog a name?" Mark asked. He shook his head. "Bad idea. You can't keep it, you know."

"Why 'Duke'?" Connor asked, ignoring Mark's comment.

"Look at him," I said, pointing back at Duke.

Connor turned around. Duke trotted along behind us, head held high, as if admiring his subjects.

"He certainly does act like he owns the street." Connor laughed.

"He's a royal, I just know it," I said. Duke came up to my outstretched hand. I petted his head.

"Just be careful with him, Adrianna. He could have fleas," Mark warned, setting down the camera tripod under a shady tree. He checked his watch again and scanned the street. "Well, we should be getting picked up soon. I'm gonna go get something nice and cold to drink—you in, Connor?"

"I am indeed in." Connor nodded.

"Adrianna, do you want anything?" Mark asked.

I shook my head. "No, I'm okay. I can stay with the stuff while you guys go inside." I sat down next to the tripod. Duke planted himself next to my foot with a sigh. I smiled at him, proud of the shots we had just done. Mark and Connor had applauded my narrations and said I was a natural in front of the camera. I couldn't wait to tell Mom and Dad.

Squinting into the bright sun, I suddenly spotted two dogs running down the street toward me. A large man with bushy red hair chased after them.

"*¡Oye! ¡Regresa aquí!* Get back here, you mutts!" he yelled as they tore down the dirt road. The two dogs, obviously strays, paused by where Duke and I were and looked back to see the man heaving to catch his breath. He waved his arms, which made the dogs bark in fear and start running again.

It was only when he stopped to pant that I saw what his shirt said . . . but I should've guessed it already. EMPLEADO DE LA PERRERA. Dogcatcher. Duke gave a soft whine and hid behind my legs as the man got closer. Did he know this dogcatcher? Had he been chased before?

The whining caught the dogcatcher's attention and he looked over at us. *"Hola pequeña. ¿Ese es tu perro?"*

I nodded. "Yes. *Es mío,*" I squeaked out.

He looked at me like he didn't believe me. It was probably obvious I was lying since Duke was covered in dirt. But the man gave me a single nod back and said, "You better put a collar on him, then. Don't want me, or any other dogcatcher, to think he's a stray."

He looked at where the other dogs had disappeared and shook his head, throwing his hands up in frustration. "*Cuídate,* little one," he said, and walked away.

I let out a big gasp of air I didn't know I had been holding. Let Duke be captured by *that* guy?! No way! Suddenly, a black van with WILD SURVIVAL!

printed on its side parked across the street. Alice, who was driving, honked the horn and waved at me, rolling down the window.

"Hey, Adrianna! Where is everyone?" she asked.

Still shaken up, I pointed to the store behind us. Her face lit up.

"Oh, perfect! I need a quick drink. Why don't you climb inside? The air is on, so it's nice and cool in here." Alice rolled the window back up and jumped out of the van. She went into the *tienda*, leaving Duke and me alone outside.

I stayed exactly where I was and looked down at Duke. He looked back up at me with soulful brown eyes.

I couldn't let the dogcatcher throw sweet Duke in doggy prison. I bent down to pet Duke, and a lightbulb suddenly went off over my head. Feye and I had *always* wanted a puppy. Maybe if I surprised him with Duke, he'd forgive me and we'd also have a new family member!

"Come on, Duke! We're getting you out of here," I whispered, standing up and hurrying over to the van. I opened the back of the vehicle and saw a bunch of large plastic tubs that the camera crew used for gear. I grabbed a nearby roll of duct tape and the trusty Sharpie pen that was always near the tape, and wrote *FRAGILE* on a long silvery strip before ripping it with my teeth and placing it on top of one of the plastic tubs' lids.

I quickly peeked around the side of the van's door toward the store to make sure no one was coming out yet. Coast was clear!

"All right, Duke. Jump up! Come on," I said, patting the clear spot near the tub. Being the clever boy he was, Duke jumped up and sat next to the ratty tub. It was full of holes from years of use. Perfect for Duke to be able to breathe! "Such a good boy," I said as I kissed his nose.

"Okay, now here." I pointed to the tub, and he jumped into it. I took the plastic bag of treats from my pocket and emptied the remainder of them into the tub. "You need to be real quiet, understand? We're going to get you on set and then I'll sneak you into the boat hotel. But you need to be very quiet." I put my finger to my lips and rubbed his head before putting the lid on top.

I shut the door just as they all emerged from the shop.

"Where did the dog go?" Connor asked, staring at me as he climbed into the front seat.

I shrugged. "He ran off after a dogcatcher scared him," I said. My stomach twisted into knots. I hated lying, especially to adults.

"Oh," Connor said, shoulders sagging.

"You couldn't have kept him anyway," Mark said.

Connor grumbled something under his breath.

"Buckle up, everyone!" Alice called over her shoulder, starting the van.

I fastened my seat belt and patted the tub with Duke next to me. I crossed my fingers and took a deep breath. Operation Dog Rescue was underway!

CHAPTER ELEVEN

The ride to the dock was a short and uneventful one, just like I hoped it would be. As the adults talked about the shots they had completed that day, I concentrated on making sure Duke didn't bark loudly for attention. I was worried he was going to get lonely and make noise, but thankfully he stayed quiet. *Phew!* Once the van parked at the dock and everyone started loading up the plastic tubs into the boat that would take us back to the hotel, I began to worry all over again.

Mentally, I crossed my fingers and toes that he would stay quiet. I let out a big sigh of relief when I saw that the plastic tub labeled *FRAGILE* was still intact and safely loaded up. Then I joined Alice, Mark, and Connor at the front of the boat to collect a sandwich snack. We ate a lot of sandwiches during TV shoots.

I grabbed my food and sat down close to the boxes as the boat engine roared to life. I made sure everyone was busy eating before I sneaked over to see how Duke was doing.

"Duke?" I half whispered. Silence.

"Duke?" I asked, a little louder this time.

A small whining noise was my answer. I quickly lifted the lid and saw a pair of eager brown eyes right in my face. I laughed as he licked my chin.

"Hey! You can't have cheese. But here, have some chicken," I whispered, digging into my sandwich and taking out the meat.

He chowed down in silence, and I sat next to him, my fingers digging into his scruffy shoulders. His tail wagged in appreciation. When he finished his snack, he lay down and let me continue petting him.

Laughter from inside the front section of the boat startled Duke and me, causing him to bark.

"What was that?" I heard someone say from inside.

Uh-oh!

"Come on, Duke, back in the tub. You gotta hide," I said, pushing him toward the box. Reluctantly, he obeyed and climbed back in, eyes big and sad as I carefully placed the lid on top of the tub once more.

"Adrianna?" I heard just as I'd finished.

I whirled around to find Connor there, looking at me with an arched eyebrow.

"What are you doing out here with all of the stuff?" he asked.

Quick, Adrianna, think of something!

"I . . . uh . . . thought I left my sunglasses out

here. Mom wouldn't be happy if I lost another pair—my second in a month!" I said, shrugging.

"Uh-huh." He looked confused. "Well, we can look for them later. Being out here with all these heavy boxes on a moving boat is a bad idea."

He stretched out his hand and I took it, allowing myself to be helped back to the front of the boat. "Hey, you're getting pretty good with your animal noises, by the way," Connor said.

"Huh?" I asked. Connor and I had a game where we would give each other an animal to try to mimic. I was especially proud of my elephant noises.

"Your dog barking just now. Perfect! I almost believed a stray had sneaked on," he said.

I smiled sheepishly. "Ha. Wouldn't that be something."

I sat down with everyone at the front and tried to think of something to change the subject. It was then that I remembered the poachers I had seen.

"Hey, Mark? Alice? Connor? I have to tell you something," I said, unsure of what they would even be able to do after I told them.

"What's up, Adrianna?" asked Alice, sensing the seriousness in my voice.

"You know the 'wanted' posters we saw at the farm? Of all the poachers?" I asked.

They all nodded.

"I saw two of them—those poachers that Soriano said were super dangerous. They're here! And I heard them saying if they didn't get 'this monster' soon, they'd be in big trouble," I continued. "We have to tell someone!"

"Are you sure it was the people from the poster?" Connor asked.

It was my turn to nod. "Yeah. They looked exactly like the photos on the poster. I'm sure of it."

"We should tell Savage when we get back," Mark

muttered, almost to himself. He looked over at Alice. "He should be able to tell the authorities, no?"

Alice shrugged. "No clue of the protocol for this. But it wouldn't hurt to ask." She turned back to me. "You did really well letting us know. We'll take care of it, okay?"

I flashed her a small smile. I had helped—twice in one day! Surely that would earn me some brownie points for getting back onto the show, right?

Before I knew it, we were pulling into the dock at the boat hotel. I watched uneasily as the crew unloaded the plastic tubs onto the shore. So far Duke had been a good boy and not made a peep.

But I realized I hadn't thought this plan through. Would I be able to sneak him all the way up to my room? What was I going to do with him once I got him up there?

CHAPTER TWELVE

Step one: Sneak Duke up the stairs and to my room. Step two: Find the dog treats Connor had left over from our "Dogs of Cuba" segment.

It felt like an eternity passed until everyone left the loading dock area, but once the coast was clear, I rushed to the box and peered inside. Duke was lying on his side, and his ears perked up at the sight of me.

"Hi, boy. Oh, what a perfect boy you are!" I smiled, petting his sides and giving him kisses on his face.

"I'm gonna sneak you up to my room, okay?" I whispered into his fur. I lifted him out of the box and tiptoed over to the stairs to the second floor. I could hear some of the crew in the kitchen, and some of them in the dining room near the stairs. I closed my eyes and listened for anyone walking above us. Nothing. Now was my chance!

"Come on, Duke! Follow me," I said, and waved for him to follow me. We took the stairs quickly and practically ran into my room. I slammed the door behind us.

Phew! I did it! Gratefully, I slid down the door and breathed a sigh of relief.

From over on my bed, Duke whined.

"You hungry, Duke?" I asked. He stuck out his tongue and his tail wagged in response. Hungry it was!

"Okay, I'll see what I can find," I said.

I stood up and exited my room, quietly closing the door behind me. Bounding down the stairs, I was so focused on not missing a step and thinking of step two of my plan—getting Duke food—that I didn't see Connor and slammed right into him.

"Oh! I'm so sorry!" I said, holding on to the stair rail for balance. "Hey, Connor, what did you do with the bag of dog treats you had?"

"It's in my room," Connor said, then looked at me curiously. "Why?"

I shrugged. "Just wondering."

"Just wondering what?" Feye asked from the bottom of the stairs. His face was sleepy, as if he had just woken up from a nap—he could sleep anywhere. Once I found him sleeping on top of an anchor!

"Wait—" Connor started, but he couldn't finish his question. Duke had somehow escaped my room and came running over, excitedly wagging his tail.

Oops. I looked at the shocked expressions on Feye's and Connor's faces. There was a long silence.

"Surprise!" I grinned sheepishly. "I got us a pet! Well, a pet for you, Feye." I looked at my brother.

"I know we've always talked about wanting a dog and . . . well, his name is Duke."

"I thought you said he ran off?" Connor mumbled. His tone was disapproving, but I could tell he was also a little happy to see Duke again.

"I didn't want him going to *la perrera*! He doesn't belong there," I said. "I just couldn't leave him."

Feye reached down to pick Duke up. Duke gave his approval by giving him a big, slobbery kiss on the cheek.

"But we can't keep him, Adrianna. Mom and Dad are going to be furious," Feye said.

I sighed. When did Feye start sounding so responsible and adultlike?

Suddenly, we heard both my parents talking downstairs.

"I'm not telling them," Feye said. He grinned for the first time since the crocodile incident.

"Well, until you two figure something out, I'm

going to suggest keeping this pup in hiding," said Connor. "I'll grab that bag of dog treats. Just keep him quiet and safe in your room for now."

Feye turned to me, still holding Duke. "Well, if we can't find this 'Mega Croc,' maybe we can dress the little guy up as a ferocious beast." We both broke out into laughter.

CHAPTER THIRTEEN

The next day, as I walked back out to the main area, I heard my parents and Mr. Savage speaking in hushed tones.

"I'm going to be honest with you, things aren't looking good for the show," Mr. Savage said. "We haven't gotten a shot of the Mega Croc, Feye got his hand glued to a croc, Connor nearly gotten eaten by another croc . . . It's a bit of a disaster. We're running out of time, and if we don't get the right shots, we don't have a show."

Dad muttered something, but I couldn't make it out.

"This is how I pictured the show: We open up to dramatic mangrove scenery with you two whizzing out on a boat. An ominous voice talks about the Mega Croc legend in the background, and how you heard of a big injured croc that might be this legendary predator. You guys and the kids teach us about the unique wildlife of Cuba and how humans coexist with the animals here, like Adrianna's bit with the working dogs. We tag some crocs, we continue looking for this monster. And then we find it and BAM. Legend confirmed!"

"Rick, it sounds like most of that has been filmed," my mom said.

"But not the most dramatic scenes—we really need that Mega Croc to sell the show," Mr. Savage continued.

"We've told you our thoughts about this 'Mega Croc' theory you have, Rick," my dad said. "Are there some big crocs here? Yeah, definitely. But one as big as this legend? I highly doubt it. We thought this show was mainly about rescuing the injured croc."

I scurried up to Feye's room and banged on his door.

"Yes?" he asked, unamused.

"The show is in trouble and we still haven't found the injured crocodile. We should help!"

"How?"

"Can you get the maps of the area we're in that Mom and Dad are using? I only have mine and I don't think it's complete," I said.

Feye disappeared for a moment, returning with a pile of maps that he spread out on his bedroom floor. I grabbed my version of the map and handed it to him.

His map included red X's on most of the locations Mom and Dad had visited so far. Feye began drawing more red X's on each mangrove channel that our parents had explored while I was filming the dog segment. He circled the channels they were still planning to visit. We gazed at the ones that were left.

"There aren't that many to look through now, which is why Mr. Savage is worried," Feye said. "If they haven't found it yet, they think it might've died or been captured by those poachers you told Mark, Alice, and Connor about." He shrugged, looking at the notes the local guides had given them on each channel. He began drawing another X on a mangrove channel.

"What are you doing?" I asked, pointing.

"According to these notes, there is no way the crocodile could be here. The map from the locals shows there was a channel there once, but their notes say it's pretty much dried up," Feye said, waving the papers in his hand.

His attention went back to the papers, and after a few silent minutes of me staring at him while he read, he wrote another X on a channel. "The maps from today and back in the 1980s are so different that they almost don't look the same. The notes are helping me figure out what is still here and what isn't," Feye explained.

"Give me a page of notes and let me see if I can help," I said. Feye handed me a page with handwriting that was hard to read. Hard, but not impossible. Feye definitely had worse handwriting, and I could make out what he wrote most of the time. We sat there in silence for who knows how long, but at the end, we were able to cross off a few more until there were only five options left.

"Can you hand me that map of this area from the 1980s?" I asked, startling Feye. He looked through the pile of papers he had given me earlier, which I had put aside, and finally found it.

"Here!" he said, passing me the map. "What are you looking for?"

I didn't answer him, too busy scanning the map for any clues. Suddenly . . . could it be? YES! "Eureka!" I yelled, jumping up. Duke barked in protest, startling both of us. When did he get in here?!

"Look at this, Feye," I said, ignoring Duke. I'd deal with his escapades later. I went to his open window and closed it, then held the map from the 1980s up to the window's light and the current map on top of it. "This map on top is from today. The map behind is from the eighties. Do you see how there is a channel in the older map? They left one out!"

"Do you think it was done on purpose?" he asked, looking at his own copy of the map from today.

"Maybe. Before we left, I read in a book from the library about how sometimes secret channels could be used to hide from police or smuggle drugs. That might be why it got left off this map," I said.

My brother smiled. "My sister is so cool

sometimes. You cracked the mystery with your map-reading skills! We've got to tell Mom and Dad," he said.

Feye and I ran downstairs.

"Mom! Dad!" I shouted. "Feye and I found a secret mangrove channel!" Reaching the two of them and Mr. Savage at the table, I unrolled the map of the mangroves. Feye stood behind me, quiet. I looked back at him and he nodded in encouragement. "Maybe the crocodile is hiding here because not as many boats enter," I said, pointing.

Our parents looked it over and my dad smiled.

"So, what do you say? Mom? Dad?" I asked, looking at them both.

Our mom looked at the map once again and frowned. "I'm not sure. These old maps aren't always reliable . . ."

Feye backed me up. "We haven't found the injured croc anywhere else. We have to at least try."

"We don't have any evidence this channel hasn't dried up or is even there still," Dad said.

"One surefire way to check if it's there is to go and look!" Feye suggested.

Dad didn't look convinced.

"Or . . . it's a long shot . . ." I said, mostly to myself, but apparently it was loud enough for my family to look at me. "Mom, do we have any information from that crocodile we tagged earlier?" I asked.

"Well, let's take a look at the latest data." Mom took her laptop out from the backpack slung on the chair behind her. With a few taps on her keyboard, she brought up the live animal-tracking software.

"It has definitely gotten around quite a bit," Dad said, looking over Mom's shoulder.

Mr. Savage nodded, his eyes scanning the map as well.

"Are there any of those dots by this hidden

channel?" I asked. I gave Dad the hard copy maps so he and Mom could compare them to the screen.

"Maybe this crocodile was stressed after we captured it and went to the secret channel to rest," I said.

None of the adults said anything for a little bit, until Mr. Savage suddenly pointed from the maps to the laptop and let out a gasp. "They're right!"

CHAPTER FOURTEEN

"Let's go! What are we waiting for?" Mr. Savage cried, waving his hands in the air.

"Julio and I can go check it out. The kids stay," my mom said.

Mr. Savage bit his lip. "Well . . . the show is about the Villalobos family. It's in the contract. They should really come. Plus, they are the ones who found this channel."

Mom frowned again.

"Mom, Mark and Connor said Adrianna did really well with the dog segment. And she just figured out where the injured croc might be. I think she deserves to come. She's an important part of this team," Feye said.

"You're right, *mijo*," Mom said, and turned to me. "I think we just have trouble with letting our little girl grow up so quickly . . ."

I smiled. "I'll be okay, Mom. Promise."

A giant grin flashed across Feye's face. "You hear that, crew?! We're going to save an injured crocodile! Let's go!" he yelled.

We didn't waste any time launching into prep mode and loading up the boats.

I let one of the sound production crew members put a microphone down the back of my shirt. Mom decided to take this opportunity to slather reef-safe sunscreen on my face, even though I hated how sticky the stuff left me. "Mo-om! It smells!" I complained, trying to get away from her white-covered hands.

"Skin cancer is no joke, *mija*. Let me put it on and rub it in well," she said.

"But why can't I wear some of the good-smelling sunscreen like the other kids I see on the beach?" I asked, frowning.

Despite my protests, Mom went ahead and put sunscreen on the back of my neck, the back of my hands, and behind my ears. *Yuck!*

Dad walked past us and scooped me up, carrying me onto the boat and setting me down near the front. He knew I loved the front of the boat.

"All right, we all ready?" Mr. Savage asked both our boats as he peered at us from the dock where he stood. *"¡Estamos listos!"* we all said in unison.

Mr. Savage fist pumped the air. "Awesome! I'll be with the film production crew in this second boat and follow you all." Mr. Savage turned to one of the camera people as he walked away from our boat and said, "Let's see if we can get a drone up to follow us for some cool aerial shots. Can we do that?" We didn't get to hear the answer to that question.

With the roar of the engine, we were off! It felt so good to feel waves pounding beneath the boat as we sped up and out of our main channel. The air was spiced with sea salt and I breathed it in.

We slowed down to go around a bend and I spotted a snake slithering across the water and up the roots of a mangrove tree. It was a creamy brown color. I would have missed it had it not been moving so quickly up the tree. Was it looking for an egg to feast on? I looked high up the treetop to see if I could spot a bird's nest and found none. The multiple greens of the leaves on the mangrove trees were a beautiful contrast against the now–deep purple sky. I hadn't noticed that the sun had begun to dip down below the horizon—we were running out of time to find our injured croc! I glanced back down to see if I could spot the snake again, but its camouflage was just too good.

I looked down into the water at the maze of

mangrove roots. Schools of fish darted through them as our boat passed by.

"Oh, wow, look at that!" Feye yelled, and the boat came to a standstill as the captain killed the engine. It was quiet enough that you could hear the crickets and nighttime bugs coming out to sing their hellos. We all followed Feye's pointed finger up to the canopy of a mangrove tree that had some rustling leaves.

Suddenly, a large creature appeared on a branch. It looked like a cross between a rat and a capybara. It clutched mangrove leaves in its paw as it stared at us and stopped its munching. We stayed quiet, not wanting to spook it. It tore its eyes away from us to continue feasting.

"What is that?" Feye asked to no one in particular.

By this time, the other boat had caught up to us

and one of their boat crew members spoke up. "It's a hutia! It's either a Desmarest's hutia or a prehensile-tailed hutia. Both are pretty common here in the Caribbean."

"Why would they nest up there? Wouldn't they fall?" I asked.

"No, it is too dangerous here for them to burrow underground. Not only do they get hunted by boas and crocodiles, but humans, too," the crew member said.

"You *eat* them?" Feye said. He looked back at the hutia, which was now making its way noisily through the canopy and out of our sight.

"Yup, in a large pot with some wild nuts and honey. They are really delicious."

It reminded me of how in Ecuador we went to a family friend's farm and they gave us guinea pig to eat. I tried it, so our parents wouldn't say I was being

HUTIA

- Hutias are a large species of rodent.
- They have short limbs, large heads, and abundant whiskers.
- Hutias are very good climbers. They have strong claws that let them scale trees.

rude, but it was not my favorite meal. I couldn't look any guinea pigs in the eye for a good few months after!

"It's gone now. We need to get going to find this channel before the sun goes down," Mom said. The boat came to life once more as the captain thrust us forward. The sky was now being kissed with shades of orange and red.

I was paying such close attention to the bulging mangrove treetops to look for more hutias that it was easy to spot when there were a few trees missing. Their absence made a clear divot in the otherwise-plump tree line.

"There!" I screamed over the roar of the boat engine as we came across a very narrow opening—the secret channel!

"Good spotting, Adrianna!" Feye celebrated, giving me a high five. As the boats made their way carefully up the hidden passageway, our parents motioned to turn the boat engines off so as not to scare any of the animals away.

Our family split up, so we were on both sides of the boat, looking for signs of a crocodile on the muddy banks of the mangroves. I looked out for anything that looked like a floating log in the water, or slide marks, drag marks, and flattened vegetation that crocodiles leave behind when they have been on the banks recently.

After twenty minutes of looking, I heard Dad sigh and run a muddied hand through his hair. He was frustrated . . . we all were.

I knew that Dad was about to suggest we turn around and give up on this channel when I suddenly saw his eyes brighten. He took a few steps forward and frantically began pointing at some slide tracks—they were of a crocodile! And they looked fresh! The captains of each boat slowly got closer until a hissing noise stopped everyone in their tracks.

"Everyone quiet! Do you hear that?" Mr. Savage asked from the film production boat behind us. "Sound, make sure you capture that hissing."

The sound people frantically checked their mics to make sure they were strong enough to pick it up. They nodded.

"All right, cameras, we're about to get some action. I want one on the family and one on the croc. Let's roll!" Mr. Savage directed. The camera crew hoisted their big cameras onto their shoulders.

Suddenly, it seemed like the air around us was devoid of life. Not even the bugs were chirping anymore. Only the soft hum of cameras, our breathing, and the lapping of the water against our boats could be heard. But finally, we heard that familiar sound again! I looked over at my brother and he nodded at me. We knew what that hissing meant. It took everything in me not to squeal out loud.

"Crocodiles sometimes make a hissing noise

when they feel threatened, meaning we're close," Feye whispered to one of the cameras. Mark gave us a thumbs-up. Feye and I turned to each other and smiled.

"There! I see it!" Mom said. The camera's attention quickly went from us to our parents. Piercing reptilian eyes looked at us, and suddenly, everyone was able to see the massive crocodile as it hauled itself out of the water a little bit more, water running down its scaly sides. Covered in mud, it blended in perfectly with the surrounding murky water until it opened its mouth to reveal its pale pink tongue and numerous dirty teeth, ready to snap at us if we came any closer. Its back leg was clearly mangled. This was the croc we had been looking for!

The yellow eyes met mine. Chills ran down my back.

"Are you okay?" Feye was suddenly at my side.

I looked up at him and nodded, reaching out for

his hand, giving it a good squeeze. "Yeah. Thanks, Feye," I whispered back. I wasn't scared of the crocodile, really. More in awe of it.

"Julio, do you have the tranquilizer?" Mom asked, ignoring the cameras that were now trying to get the best angle to capture both our mother and the crocodile in the same shot.

"Give me one . . . second . . . almost . . . there . . . done! Locked and loaded, fire when ready, *mi amor*," Dad said, handing the tranquilizing gun over. We took a step back—we knew our mother didn't like us being near her when she fired the tranquilizer gun.

Thwap! She hit her mark, and the crocodile thrashed around in the shallow, muddy bank as the tranquilizer began to take effect. It tried to climb out of the muddy hole it was in, but with such a badly injured leg it wasn't possible.

"Are you getting this, Mark?" Mr. Savage asked, and Mark zoomed in on the crocodile in the hole.

After a few minutes, it went still, and our parents rushed out of the boat to check on it. Some of the cameras followed, but Mark stayed behind to film the action that would soon take place on the boat. Now that we had found the injured croc, we'd be taking it back with us to assess its injuries.

"It's down! All right, Adrianna, get the boat ready. Feye, hand me the duct tape," Dad said.

As Feye jumped down to hand them the tape, Mark filmed me as I cleared the back of the boat and began to lay down large towels. Although most of a crocodile's skin is thick, similar to armor, and covered with rugged scales called osteoderms that provide protection for them on top, they have smooth skin on their bellies and sides, which makes those areas more vulnerable. The team would be moving the large crocodile onto a stretcher to provide some extra padding underneath, and then bringing it over to the boat. I wanted to make sure this beautiful predator didn't get hurt any further as we tried to take care of it.

As I cleared the boat of anything sharp, our parents duct-taped the mouth of the crocodile shut. They were careful to make sure they didn't cover the nostrils so it could still breathe. Feye brought out his measuring tape from his pocket. Mom held one end of the measuring tape by the snout, and Feye made his way down to the tail.

Feye let out a whistle. "Wow, a big one! Thirteen feet!"

The high end of length for American crocodiles was usually fifteen feet, so this was a really big one! I gently hopped off the boat and went to pick up the croc stretcher so I could bring it over to my family. I had pure adrenaline pumping through my veins now.

"Adrianna, are you sure you can handle the stretcher by yourself?" Mr. Savage asked from the boat. He had momentarily stopped giving directions to the sound and camera crew to look at me.

I nodded. "I'm good." I wanted to prove I could do this.

"All right, kiddo. Just be careful," Mr. Savage said. He turned his attention back to his clipboard, which had notes about how he wanted the scene to be captured. I picked up the stretcher and let the back part drag behind me as I walked toward my family.

"We'll do more data collection and analysis once we've got the croc on the boat. Right now, we've got to get it out of here and clean that wound with water and antiseptics," Mom said into the camera.

I handed the stretcher over to my dad. Together he, Mom, and a few of the crew members wiggled it under the massive predator while others rocked the crocodile back and forth to make room for the stretcher.

Feye made his way back to the boat, and I saw Mark zoom in on him as he dialed the Wildlife Hospital back at Sacred Sanctuary and Zoological Park on our satellite phone. "Hey! Martha, can you hear me? It's Feye. We've got a thirteen-foot American crocodile with a badly injured hind leg. We'll be there in about . . ." He looked over to Mr. Savage to get a time.

"Tell them forty-eight hours, kid!" Mr. Savage replied as he directed cameras to capture a variety of shots.

I had been so preoccupied bringing the stretcher to my family and watching my brother going back to the boat that I hadn't realized Mr. Savage had gotten off the production boat. Most likely to see what the cameras were capturing and to give them more directions of angles he wanted. I watched him as he stood by the hole that the crocodile was in.

As our parents and the crew members stumbled up out of the hole with the crocodile stretcher and then across the muddy terrain of the mangroves back to the boat, Mr. Savage poked at a muddy lump with the toe of his boot. An expression of surprise crossed his face, and he quickly smoothed the mud back over with his boot.

That's weird . . . I thought. *Why is he playing around in the mud?*

But there were soon more exciting things happening. I turned my attention to my parents loading the injured crocodile onto our boat. I turned back to look at Mr. Savage, who was now moving toward us, asking the cameras to focus on certain parts of the crocodile, like its closed eyes.

It was then that I noticed a bright yellow field notebook at the base of the tree where Mr. Savage had been standing. I was about to say something when our dad came over and gave me and Feye a big hug.

"Good job, *mijos*." Dad then looked at the camera and said, "Now, time to get out of here and get back home to save this croc."

CHAPTER FIFTEEN

"Hold up," Mark said before our engines started. He was looking down at his tablet where drone footage was displayed. "I can see another croc moving just north of here, and it looks massive!" Everyone stilled for a second.

Then Mr. Savage's voice boomed behind us as he stormed down the bank.

"New plan, everyone. Connor, I want you and a couple of the crew to take the boat with our injured croc and make sure it makes it back to home base in good condition. The Villalobos, cameras, and safety divers come with us. We're finally going to capture this Mega Croc on tape!"

My mom looked uneasy. "Rick, we should make sure the kids and this croc get back safely. Plus, the sun has set. They've only dived at night a handful of times."

"This may be THE shot, so I think it's crucial the entire family gets in on this. We'll make sure everyone stays safe. I promise."

I looked over at Mom and Dad hopefully.

My mom sighed and looked at Dad. "I don't really like this, Julio . . ."

Dad ran his hands through his hair. "This could be a really pivotal shot. And I think the kids can handle it. They've more than proved that they can take this seriously and follow directions." He smiled warmly at me.

Mom turned back to me. "You are still grounded, *señorita,* even though you have been quite responsible lately and we are proud of you for that. If Mr. Savage insists you're in the shot, then it's your lucky day," she said.

I was nervous. Not to be around the crocodile necessarily. I knew from my research that the American crocodile wasn't as aggressive as other types, but I didn't exactly love night diving. Speeding toward the area with this new crocodile, Mr. Savage turned to some of the boat crew, including the safety divers. "You're in there only a few minutes, max, because it is dark. Are we ready?" The safety divers nodded.

"Let's film what may be the highlight of this episode!" Mr. Savage said as he clapped his hands.

Mark confirmed when we'd reached the spot he'd seen an American crocodile on the drone footage. As the boat slowed to a stop, some of the camera people began descending into the water. After a few minutes, one yelled out, "We see it!"

Mr. Savage clapped his hands again. "I want one safety diver for each family member. Let's get you all in the water."

We all kissed one another's cheeks and one by one got ready and then slipped under the water.

Outside of the spotlights the camera crew had set up, the water was completely dark. I felt as though I'd just dove into outer space.

The safety diver assigned to me tapped my shoulder, checking in with me. I gave him the "okay" sign, a bit nervous. A few seconds later he pointed behind me and turned me around.

It was then that I saw the American crocodile. Easily ten feet long, it looked like a prehistoric dinosaur slowly swimming toward our family. It was big, but not "mega."

The underwater cameras and lights immediately lit up the crocodile's face. I saw my parents talking into cameras and pointing out the crocodile.

AMERICAN CROCODILE

- American crocodiles eat a wide variety of foods, including crabs, turtles, fish, and snakes.
- Like Cuban rock iguanas, crocodiles like to bask in the sun to help raise their body temperature. Sometimes they sun themselves with their mouths open to help regulate temperature.
- Temperature plays a big role in determining the sex of crocodile embryos. If crocodile eggs are incubated at a temperature of 88 degrees or higher, the resulting baby crocodiles will be mostly male; at temperatures below 88 degrees, the baby crocodiles will be mostly female.

Both Feye and I stayed back, observing. After a few more minutes, the crocodile left the hectic scene in the lights and was swallowed by the inky darkness.

I suddenly heard a crackling sound in my ears. The sound of my parents' voices abruptly cut out. *Uh-oh.* I swam toward the lights and pointed at my ears, signaling to my safety diver that there was a problem. I watched his blurry figure swim away, letting someone else know.

After a minute he returned, giving me a thumbs-up and then the "dive over" signal with his hands to say the dive was over. I gave him the "okay" sign, ready to warm up with some hot cocoa back at the boat hotel. As he swam in front of me, I stayed down for a few extra seconds so his fins wouldn't hit me in the face.

The camera crew disappeared above me in slow motion. With the warm thought of marshmallows in my head, I kicked my legs toward the surface. Night diving was always fascinating, but I much preferred sunlit dives in broad daylight!

But my thoughts were abruptly interrupted by a sudden sharp pain in my left leg. *What was that?* I looked down, trying to see if my suit had gotten caught on a gnarled mangrove root, but all I could see was inky darkness.

I kicked my leg to try to free it from whatever had snagged it—but another jolt of pain shot throughout my body. My stomach dropped. This was no tree root. Before I knew it, I was being pulled away from the surface and into the depths of the muddy seafloor below.

CHAPTER SIXTEEN

I clawed at the sand, stirring up clouds of grainy dust that made it impossible to see. Desperately, I tried to see if I could grab on to a rock or something to keep from being dragged too far away.

Because it was clear now: I was being dragged by a massive American crocodile who had half my leg clamped firmly in its jaws. I took a quick glance back and tried not to cry as I realized how much trouble I was in. *Whatever you do, A, don't move that leg!* screamed my inner voice as my fingers raked through the mangroves' silty bottom.

I'd grown up surrounded by wild animals. I

knew what often happened in these scenarios: a person did not survive. I had never heard of someone being bitten while scuba diving, so this was new territory for me.

Play dead, A. Don't let it think of you as food, my inner voice returned, a little quieter. If I moved too much, the predator could bite down harder, making this an extremely painful situation to be in. Or worse, it could launch into one of the infamous crocodile death rolls.

My mind went back to the one time I had seen a crocodile at the zoo do a death roll. The large male tensed up like a sprinter before a race. Then it exploded into action, using its hind legs to roll over and over again until the animal in its teeth was long dead.

If the croc holding on to me now did either of those things, I would surely lose my leg . . . or my life.

I took a deep breath and closed my eyes for a

split second to think. I remembered what Dad had told Feye when his hand had gotten stuck to the crocodile tag. "Keep breathing. It's important to stay calm."

I opened my eyes again. I was a little calmer now. I stopped raking my hands through the silty soil. I remembered now that mangroves usually didn't have big rocks lying around in the sand. What I needed to do was try to call for help. The fancy scuba diving mask I was wearing had a microphone. Even though it had been acting up before and I couldn't hear anyone else . . . maybe they could still hear me. I jammed my finger on the microphone button and hoped for the best.

"Guys, the crocodile has got me! I'm being dragged!"

There was no response other than static. But hopefully my message had gone through. I turned my attention back to controlling my breathing.

Don't freak out, Adrianna. The croc is just curious. Right? Breathe. You just got a new tank of oxygen before starting this dive, and if you keep calm and breathe like normal, you'll have plenty of air. Breathe.

Just as I began to rack my brain to think of what else I could do, I suddenly felt the pressure on my leg release. The crocodile had let go of my leg!

I didn't hesitate. I filled my scuba diving vest up with air and shot to the water's surface. I flew up quickly, as if I were strapped to a rocket, not caring about doing the safety stop I would have taken normally to help my body adjust to the pressure. No way was I staying in the water for five more minutes!

Surfacing above the water, I felt a surge of relief. But I had no idea of the level of panic and confusion that was waiting for me above the waves.

"Mom! It's Adrianna! She's over there!" I heard Feye yell as I desperately tried to get the full-face mask off.

My hands were shaking, and the thick gloves I had on were making it hard to grab the straps to loosen the mask. I thought I heard a dog barking. Duke? That wasn't possible. I must be starting to hallucinate.

"Mark! Get over there!" That was my mom's voice.

"You've got her?!" My dad.

I was suddenly surrounded by the crew members. Mark swam behind me to shield me with his giant, heavy camera. Another diver grabbed the back of my tank and started pulling me closer to the boat.

Everything began to get hazy. I looked up at the stars—I had no idea how long I was staring up at them until I saw the crew's medic, Miguel, and his *azul* eyes looking down at me. He said something, but I couldn't make out what it was as my eyelids began to droop. Miguel shook me by the shoulders and that seemed to do the trick.

Finally, I could make out what he was saying. "You're going to be okay."

I could tell he was scared. I was, too.

Without warning, I was lifted out of the water. I could hear Miguel asking for his medic bag over more barking. That was definitely Duke!

But before I could ask about him, someone piled towels on me. My mom knelt down next to me.

"*Mi nena!* Is she okay?!" my mom asked, wrapping me in a careful hug after people took off my scuba vest and tank. Miguel responded only by cutting into my dive suit and ripping the fabric open.

There, on my left leg, was the perfect imprint of the crocodile's jaw. Where each tooth had gripped me were angry, gaping wounds that now oozed bright red blood against my paling skin. I couldn't take my eyes off the marks. Was that really my leg?

Miguel blocked my view of my leg and began to ask me questions. I was about to answer when I heard someone say, "It's at the surface! The crocodile is at the surface and *looking* at Adrianna!"

A spotlight was pointed somewhere close in the water. Looking around Miguel, I could see the large crocodile staring me down, as if it was trying to say something to me.

"Mr. Savage, no!" I heard my brother yell.

Then a sudden loud BANG! noise startled everyone into silence. I turned my head to see Mr. Savage holding a hunting shotgun in his hand. Feye stood nearby, horrified.

I looked back to find the crocodile, only to see a bright red spot on its head. Its eyes were now empty of any message. I felt like screaming and tried to get up, but crew members around me made sure I didn't move.

"She's going into shock!" a voice called.

I closed my eyes, and the darkness took over.

CHAPTER SEVENTEEN

My eyelids felt like boulders. I could hear people furiously whispering near me.

First, I recognized Mr. Savage's voice. "I did what I had to do to protect your kid. You saw how it was coming back around! It could have killed her—or another crew member."

Next, I heard my mother, her voice terse and low. "We *do not* shoot animals for behaving the way they naturally do. You and I both know that if the crocodile had wanted to kill Adrianna it very easily could have."

"So, you're really trying to tell me it didn't want to kill her?"

"Crocodiles have the most powerful jaws of any animal, Rick," my dad answered. "You saw her leg. Puncture wounds and bruises—but she still *has a leg*. Thank god. As terrifying as this was for us, the crocodile was just doing what crocodiles do. This was an exploratory bite—it was trying to figure out what she was."

"What I want to know is what happened with her microphone and why her safety diver didn't stay with her," I heard mom say.

"Miguel and I have been questioning the safety diver. I believe Connor is looking into the mask and what could have happened—a wire may have come loose," Mr. Savage responded.

"I think the croc probably got twisted around with all of our bright lights," Feye interjected. "It bumped into Adrianna's leg and took a nibble to see if she was food. Clearly she tastes bad."

"Feye, *basta*. Your sister is injured. This isn't time to make jokes," Mom said.

I had had enough. I finally managed to wrench open my eyes—it took so much effort! I was in my bed in the boat hotel. My throat felt dry, but I needed to speak. "I do taste bad," I managed to croak out. The four people in the room turned to look at me, and they all smiled. And there was Duke! He sat near the foot of my bed, tongue wagging.

"Good to see you awake, kiddo. I'll ask Miguel to come take a look at that leg of yours." Mr. Savage winked and left my room, closing the door behind him.

"*Mija*, how do you feel?" Dad asked.

"Sore," I managed. "And I'm angry with Mr. Savage. He shouldn't have shot the crocodile!" My hands bunched into fists under the blankets. I wanted to ask about what they had done with the crocodile, if it had really died. I made a motion to get out of bed, but my dad gave me his famous "Do not try me right now, Adrianna Villalobos" face. I stayed put, frowning. Walking might not be in the cards just yet.

"I'm okay, Dad. Really. My leg doesn't even hurt that much," I said, trying to convince myself and him. I lifted the blanket to look at my leg for the first time. Under my knee was a kaleidoscope of bruise colors—black, blue, green, yellow—and a set of round puncture wounds in the shape of an arc. This was where the teeth of the crocodile had gone right through the wet suit and into my leg. I shuddered. It felt like a bad dream, but seeing it there meant it had all been real. I ran my hand lightly over the bites and flinched at the touch.

"I wouldn't touch that just yet if I were you, Adrianna," Miguel said as he entered the room and saw my hand near the bruises. "It's a nasty bite, but thankfully we have everything we need to take care of you right here on the boat hotel. That's why you aren't in a hospital."

"Can I try walking?" I asked. I was never one for sitting still, and I had no idea how long I had been sleeping. Just a night? A few days?

"Let's start by just standing up, little warrior," Miguel joked. "But first, I need to clean everything out again." He leaned over my leg and began to pour some kind of liquid over it. "This is going to sting a little bit," he said.

A little bit! This was more painful than actually getting bitten!

"Do you remember us washing the bite when it first happened?" Miguel asked.

Suddenly, my mind flashed back to a lot of bright lights—and a lot of pain.

Miguel had used a bleach-and-water mixture called Dakin's solution in my bite wound. I remembered now that it had felt like my leg was on fire.

I nodded at Miguel. "I remember bits and pieces of the night the crocodile bit me. I remember it hurt a lot when you cleaned it. How long have I been out?"

"Just two days," Miguel said while he was busy looking at my leg. "Well, it seems the Dakin's solution worked, even though it hurt, because I'm happy to say you don't have any signs of infection!"

"Can she try standing now?" Feye asked Miguel.

"Are you in pain?" Miguel asked.

I touched my bare leg and winced.

"It hurts when I touch it. But it doesn't feel super bad if nothing is rubbing up against it," I replied.

"Well, let's see you give it a try, then." Miguel motioned for me to try to stand. I took the hand he offered and put my right foot down on the cool tile floor. I slowly moved my left leg off the bed and lowered it down to meet my right leg. I took a deep breath.

"Is it always going to be this painful, Miguel?" I looked up at him, nervous.

"It's perfectly normal if it hurts for now. We're going to keep taking care of it, and you're going to feel a little bit better every day."

I nodded and then stood up. The leg felt sore, like I had been kicked hard, but I didn't cry out in pain.

"Hey! You're standing!" Feye clapped. Everyone else clapped, too, big smiles on their faces.

I took a few steps, walking slowly toward the door and my family.

Miguel laughed. "Whoa there! You can't go off running a half marathon!"

I looked back and grinned at him.

"I don't want you doing too much work just yet.

So, you're to take it easy for a few more days, okay?" he said.

"Look, I'm fine!" I insisted. I took a few more steps toward the door. But suddenly, I felt flushed and light-headed. Unsteadily, I turned back around. Miguel and my dad each took one of my elbows and guided me back into bed. My stomach flip-flopped as Miguel began to rebandage my leg.

"That was a good start, Adrianna," my mom whispered, smoothing the hair out of my eyes. "For now, you just need to get some rest." I looked over at my dad and Feye, who were now at the foot of my bed near Duke, who let out a little bark.

I looked at my parents and gave them a cheesy grin. "Surprise, I got us a pet!"

"Oh, Connor told us," Dad said. He sat on my bed and looked at Duke. "The dog hasn't left your side this entire time while you've been sleeping."

I smiled at Duke. "Good boy."

I turned back to my family. "Did he get on one of the boats? I heard him barking, after I got bit."

Feye shook his head. "No, Adrianna. He was here the whole time."

Huh . . . so I had been hallucinating.

"Can we keep him?" I asked my mom.

"We can't keep him, Adrianna. We travel too much for work to keep a dog," Mom explained.

I sighed.

Mom saw my face and came to kiss my forehead. "We can discuss it more later. Duke can stay, for now. You'll need him to entertain you during these next few days of recovery."

"I can stay with you tonight, A, if you want. So you aren't too bored," Feye offered, and I nodded. "Although I can't imagine you being bored with this stowaway dog."

"What about the injured croc? Don't we need to get it back to the zoo?" I asked, suddenly worried. I didn't want my injury to make the croc's situation worse!

"She's doing great. We were able to stabilize her with our equipment here. We may have one of us head back with her and the other stay here until you're healed enough to travel. But don't worry about that for now," my mom said.

"And the show? Is it going to be okay?"

"That's to be determined," my dad said. "We don't know if the network wants to air a young girl getting bitten by a croc, or the aftermath of Mr. Savage's choices. But all that matters right now is your health." He tried to sound calm and reassuring, but I could tell he was worried.

Duke then snuggled up against my good side, and it took so much effort to put my hand up to pet him. Through heavy-lidded eyes, I watched Miguel hook me up to an IV.

CHAPTER EIGHTEEN

I crumpled up a piece of paper and aimed it at my brother's unsuspecting head, which was directly across from my bed. Feye had his headphones on blasting loud music and let out a yelp when the paper ball hit the side of his head. I laughed and made the motion for him to take a headphone off.

"Yes, Adrianna?" he asked, unamused.

"I want to go see the rescued crocodile." I was so tired of being in bed all the time. "It's our last full day here, and I don't want to be stuck in here all day!"

"Nope, I'm on strict orders to make sure you stay put and don't throw up again."

"First of all, I didn't throw up. I almost did. There's a difference. Second, you don't have to be with me—you could be out with Mom or Dad."

"Yeah . . . but then what kind of brother would I be?"

I smiled. My brother, loyal to the end. "Come on, just help me get out of bed." He rolled his eyes but came over and offered his hand.

I pushed myself back on my butt with my arms and grabbed ahold of his hand.

"You sure you're okay?" Feye asked, looking at me with worry.

I nodded, took a deep breath, and pulled myself up.

"Adrianna what are you doing out of bed?" Miguel asked, somehow immediately appearing in the doorway. He must have had a psychic sense I was getting antsy. He came in and held a hand to my forehead to feel if I had a fever.

I shook my head. "I'm fine! I know I haven't gone down the stairs yet, but I want to try."

Miguel smirked. "You're a firecracker, kiddo. Does it hurt to walk?"

Feye let me go and I proudly showed Miguel how I was walking with only a little limp.

He clapped. "Well, if it doesn't hurt I don't see why you can't go walking around up and down the place. Just no running, please. And let me change that bandage soon!" Miguel laughed, ruffled my hair, and headed back into the hall.

Freedom! Feye and I walked toward the stairs. He went first, taking two steps down and then turning around to look at me. "I've got you," he said. "Just take this slow."

It seemed like it took forever, but finally we made it down the stairs and outside. Carefully, we made our way over to the back docking section of the hotel where the crocodile was in a large, padded container. It was a contraption of tough metal and mesh woven together so that if the crocodile woke up, she wouldn't be able to break out.

Feye filled me in on her status as Mom and Dad came by to check on her. It turned out she was in okay shape, despite her injury. That made two of us!

Once I found a safe place to sit, I watched Mom and Dad take measurements and blood samples and run a few other tests. Feye stayed close by, pacing back and forth. He looked concerned.

Once our parents were done, they closed the top part of the container with multiple latches and buttons to make sure she stayed safely inside.

"Something's not adding up," Feye said.

"Why do you say that?" I asked.

"Why would she have been just hanging out in that mud hole? That would make her an easy target for anything to eat her," he mumbled.

"Maybe she was there for another good reason,"

I said, eyes now down on my bitten leg, which was outstretched over the stair railing.

"I just don't buy it," said Feye. He continued to pace, mumbling to himself so I couldn't really understand what he was saying. I decided to ignore him unless he was actually going to tell me what was on his mind.

I focused instead on the film crew sitting at a nearby table, reviewing their video backups. I liked seeing the raw footage and watching the juicy bits of the day.

"Look at that, Feye. Pretty cool that Mom and Dad found nesting crocodiles this morning, right?" I asked. Feye nodded. "I can't believe I missed out on that because of my leg."

Feye and I watched the computer screens from nearby as the crew rewound through footage from earlier in the day. Feye and I stayed quiet as we heard the crew make jokes or write down notes about certain time stamps, and it wasn't until what felt like the fiftieth scene of nesting female crocodiles that I spotted a pattern.

"Feye," I said, grabbing my brother's leg.

"Are you okay? Do you want to go back upstairs and lie down?" he asked.

I shook my head. "No, no, I'm fine. Listen. The crocodile *was* in that muddy hole for a good reason. Why would a crocodile put her life in danger?"

Feye looked puzzled. "I don't know."

"She's a mom, Feye! That's why she was in the hole! Remember how it was at the base of a tree with a lot of leaves over a sort-of lumped-up part? Those must have been—"

"Her eggs!" we finished together.

"We've gotta tell Mom and Dad. They'll want to go back," Feye said, about to turn away when I grabbed his hand and pulled him in front of me.

"They're busy! We can totally do this on our

own—it'll be a 'Feye and Adrianna mission' just like when we were kids—" I started, but Feye put a hand up to stop me.

"You're still a kid. I'm a teen now," Feye said, puffing out his chest and winking at me. I slapped his arm.

"Listen to me, Mr. Teen! You know how to drive the boat, right?" I asked.

"Um, the dinghy, yeah. I mean I don't have my license yet, but yeah, I know how to drive the little dinghy by myself," Feye said.

"Then you can drive us there! I know where the eggs are, so if we leave now, we can get back before they're done filming for the day," I replied. "The hidden channel isn't even that far away. And I have the map right here!" I patted my vest pocket.

"Why not just wait until Mom, Dad, and the crew can join us?" Feye asked, pointing at our parents. One of the cameras was on a tripod, recording their conversation.

"We can do this by ourselves. I want them to see that I'm an important member of the team, and not just an injury machine." I gestured at my leg.

Feye still didn't look convinced.

"Every day those eggs are out in the wild, something could happen to them. They're in danger . . . Every egg counts and helps their population numbers," I explained, hoping that would persuade my brother to see how urgent it was to get these eggs as soon as possible. "Mom and Dad's wildlife collection permit allows them to safely transport eggs, too."

That seemed to do the trick. Feye sighed and slowly nodded his head.

With his hand in mine, we made our way down the stairs around to the other side of the floating hotel to where the boats were. The dinghy was at the very end and easy for us to grab and head out on.

Bark, bark! Uh-oh, it seemed Duke wanted to come along, too.

"Shhh, Duke! Be quiet!" I whispered. Duke continued to bark loudly.

Feye picked him up. "Guess he's coming with us."

The boat crew was busy running around making dinner for our last night here. No one seemed to have noticed Duke's barking, or be paying any attention to us.

Feye looked back at me and nodded to the boat. "Fifteen minutes. That's all we have. *Vamonos.*"

He helped me get into the dinghy, threw a nearby cooler for the eggs into the front of the boat, and sat himself down close to the engine. Duke settled himself next to me at the front of the boat.

Feye revved the engine enough to bring it to life but not be too loud. I untied us from the dock, and soon we were quickly but quietly making our way to the hidden mangrove channel. Once we were out of sight of the boat hotel, Feye made the engine roar for real. We whooped and hollered as we went on our first "Feye and Adrianna mission" in a long time.

"Know where we are going, A?" Feye asked over the dinghy's motor. I nodded.

"I'll tell you when to turn!" I said, confident in my navigational skills.

In the few short minutes we had spent in the boat, Feye and I were already sweating. My leg muscle spasmed, uncomfortable with the heat and sweat. It made me marvel at how mangroves could be so successful in all this heat, mud, and salt. Mangroves were clearly survivors, just like Feye had said, standing tall on mighty roots submerged underwater. *You're a survivor, too, just like them,* a voice in my head said. It sounded like my mother. I smiled.

"It's coming up, Feye! Slow down!" I shouted over my shoulder. I was going to do my part to help these crocodiles survive.

He pulled back on the gas. I pushed some of the thicker branches away from my spot at the front of the boat . . . but no secret channel revealed itself like before. It was just more mangroves. I spotted a small green Cuban tree frog sleeping on a branch, and grinned despite my frustration with our search. But where was that channel? I sighed loudly and nodded goodbye to the tree frog.

"What's the matter, A?" Feye asked, killing the engine entirely.

"This isn't it. Hold on, let me look at the map," I said. I reached down into the boat to consult the map I'd brought. But a sudden gust of wind ripped through the mangroves and pulled the map right out of my hand.

"Oh no!" I cried. I didn't even see where it landed.

Feye held up his trusty cell phone in the air. "Have no fear, Google Maps is here! I've had some luck catching a signal a few times since we've been here."

CUBAN TREE FROG

- These tree frogs are the largest in North America. They can grow up to five and a half inches long.
- The Cuban tree frog secrets a mucus from its skin that can be irritating to humans and other animals.
- They are nocturnal. They sleep on trees through the day and hunt for food at night. Their preferred meal includes creatures like spiders, cockroaches, and lizards.

He tapped his password into his phone and then held it up again. A few seconds passed and then Feye let out a sigh. This wasn't going to be one of those lucky times.

"We're lost!" Feye said, giving Duke a pat on the head. He hadn't barked once since we'd gotten on the boat.

I frowned and looked around us at the lapping water.

"No . . . we're not lost." I bent down to inspect the water at the roots of the mangroves.

"What are you doing?" Feye asked.

"Looking at the tide! To see if it's going in or out," I explained, noticing how the exposed part of the roots were a bit damp. That meant the tide was going out.

"Do you have your watch?" I asked my older brother, standing up and making my way toward him. He nodded, and I held out my hand for him to give it to me.

"You have a compass on it! I remember that on the map, the secret channel was northeast of the boat hotel."

"But my compass is wonky," Feye argued. And sure enough, it was. It was pointing north to where the sun was setting . . . and that wasn't right.

"Darn it," I said, but then looked at the sun again. "The sun sets in the west! If on your compass, north equals west, then we just have to adjust all the other directions. So, if we keep going up ahead and to the right, we should hopefully still find the hidden channel."

"I'm trusting you on this," Feye mumbled, turning the boat engine back on and puttering us up ahead slowly as I looked at the row of thick mangroves to find the secret channel.

Nope . . . nope . . . nada . . . *no, not here . . .*

Suddenly, I saw a divot in the thick mangrove branches. I let out a yelp as I almost fell forward pointing toward it. We had found the secret channel!

"You did it!" Feye said, smiling broadly. He cranked up the boat engine and we zipped toward the tree where we had found the injured mother crocodile. Duke let out a joyful bark.

"Mr. Savage dropped his bright yellow notebook near the hole," Feye said as we neared the spot where we'd picked up the crocodile. "We could use that as a guide! I saw it on the ground when we were loading up the croc."

"I saw him drop it, too!" I said. We both fell quiet as we scanned the muddy banks for a flash of yellow.

"There! I see it!" I pointed, and Feye slowed down until the dinghy slid up the muddy bank. I climbed down and out of the dinghy slowly. Feye handed me a woven bag that I had brought along, and I turned to face the pit. My shoes sunk into the mud, and I struggled to lift my legs up and out. My leg hurt, but I was surprised by how much better it felt, just a few days later. There were still foot-prints left from when we had been there earlier, so I tried stepping in those to make it easier for myself. It felt really good to be back out in the field, getting my shoes dirty, instead of lying around at the boat hotel.

I zoned in on the yellow field notebook until I was right next to it and able to pick it up. Like the field notebook Feye had, it was small and fit per-fectly in my pocket!

Feye jogged over and into the muddy depression. We both knelt down by the muddy lump at the base of the tree and began to dig with our hands. Almost immediately we saw white egg cases start to poke up out of the earth. I scooped up some mud and leaves to line the bottom of my bag with. Feye carefully placed the eggs in the bag one by one.

"Dude, why are you doing this so slowly? Just stuff them all in!" I teased my brother. It was a joke, but I also remembered Feye saying we only had fifteen minutes, tops, before we were missed. How much time had we already spent?

Feye didn't acknowledge my joke. He just handed me some more eggs, which I carefully placed on top of the ones already in the bag. We worked like that for a while, just silence outside the squelching of our shoes and the rustling of leaves. Soon the bag was almost full.

"Do you see any more, Feye?" I asked, pushing away mud to better see into the nest. Feye shook his head. "Then I think that's all of them. How many do we have?"

"Thirty-eight. Give or take an egg or two," Feye said. We both stood up to wipe the dirt off our clothes and legs. Not much good it did, though. We were completely filthy.

"Okay, let's go home!" I said.

But my brother didn't answer. He reached an arm back and gripped my arm tightly, his mouth open wide.

"Feye?" I asked.

He pointed wordlessly across the small channel in response. I followed his finger and let out a gasp.

In the murky water near our boat, two massive yellow eyes stared right at us. The yellow eyes reminded me of the crocodile that had bitten me. Could this crocodile sense that I had been bitten by another crocodile? I felt like those eyes were burning holes into my skin just like the crocodile teeth had.

Feye and I stayed perfectly still. I could already tell this was a BIG crocodile because of how far apart the yellow eyes were.

But we weren't prepared for just how big this

ancient animal was until it rose higher in the water, and we could see the end tip of its tail.

"Adrianna . . . it's longer than the boat," Feye whispered. "And the boat is fifteen feet long."

My stomach did a flip-flop. "Do you think it could be . . ." I trailed off. I couldn't say it.

Feye nodded, ever so slightly. "Adrianna, I think we're looking at the Mega Croc."

Even Duke must have known this was one animal not to bark at because he was staying very quiet. I scooted closer to Feye, and with my left hand I dug into his shorts pocket.

"What are you doing?!" he whispered, eyes darting down to me.

"Saving the show!" I hissed back at him. "This is what Mr. Savage was telling Mom and Dad we needed—video of the Mega Croc. We may not have any cameras here, but we have your phone! We can get footage of the croc!" I said.

Feye let me fish his phone out, and he grabbed it from me and turned on the camera just in time to capture the giant crocodile heaving itself out of the water and onto the bank between us and our boat.

We had big crocodiles at Sacred Sanctuary and Zoological Park, but none like this. As mud dripped off its body, we could see now that it had all the features of a Cuban crocodile, but all on a much bigger scale than usual. Its teeth were yellow, and some were broken off. I tried not to focus on its mouth, but you couldn't miss the fact that there were multiple fishing hooks in it. How much bait had it stolen in its lifetime? Even from this far, we could see some big scars on its back. And the brilliant spots Cuban crocodiles normally sported were faded with age. How old was this croc?

It paid us no mind as it made its way up the muddy bank, leaving a large drag mark from the heavy tail it pulled behind its large body. We heard branches snap in half as its humongous feet crushed them, flattening vegetation and leaving claw marks behind as it finally disappeared onto land and away from us.

Feye raised his hand up to stop the video. We had the shot! Hopefully it was good enough to save the show, but there was no time to watch it through again now. We needed to get out of here before the Mega Croc came back and decided to have a dog and two kids as an afternoon snack.

Feye and I squelched our way back to the boat as fast as my injured leg would let us. Feye helped me into the boat, gently passing me the bag of eggs before jumping back into the boat himself. Carefully, I set the bag of eggs into the cooler we'd brought with us.

"Holy guacamole. No one is going to believe this!" Feye cried out.

"Well, thankfully we have proof." I laughed, pointing to the phone in his hand.

"Glad it came in handy even without service," Feye said. He held it up and pointed it at both of us before he took a picture. "I don't want to hear you making fun of me for taking this thing everywhere ever again!"

I giggled. Suddenly, Duke began barking, a deep rumbling noise that startled us out of our conversation.

Feye glanced down the channel where we'd come from. His whole body stiffened. "What is it?" I asked.

"A boat engine. Can you hear it?" Feye whispered.

Duke continued to bark angrily. I suddenly felt like it had gotten a few degrees colder, and I shivered. I knew what we were doing was risky, and the last thing I wanted was more trouble.

CHAPTER NINETEEN

"But this is a *hidden* channel," I said. Hidden meant no one could find it, right? I mean, we went through a whole stack of maps to find it, and it was through a fluke! How many other people could have 1980s maps of these channels?

The hair on the back of my neck stood up. Something was very wrong.

"Sometimes people use these hidden channels for bad things. Like for drugs and stuff, remember?" Feye continued to whisper. "I'm getting us out of here," Feye said. He revved up the engine. It was loud. Too loud. He backed out of the muddy bank and began to slowly make his way toward our only way home. Toward the hum of another motor.

I squinted into the trees. Coming around the bend was a small white boat with black stripes running down the side, sort of like a zebra design.

Feye slowed our dinghy down and eventually turned the engine off. The channel narrowed at the entrance, and we couldn't risk bumping into another boat, no matter how eager we were to get home.

"Can you see who's in the boat?" Feye asked. I stood up on my tiptoes and spotted a woman and man near the steering wheel. They had also shut off their boat. I almost felt like we were in a western standoff, like the kind you see on TV.

"No one from the TV crew . . . It looks like . . . maybe tourists?" I said. I wasn't convinced, though. They were both wearing dark outfits. No one would plan a trip to Cuba in the summer and pack nothing but dark clothing. They even had black hats and large glasses that made me wonder if maybe they were celebrities going undercover.

"Adrianna, those do *not* look like tourists!" Feye snapped as they came closer. I knew they weren't, but a small part of me couldn't help hoping they were only harmless, lost tourists.

I noticed the man driving the boat had sun-tanned skin covered in dark tattoos. Where had I seen tattoos that looked like that before . . . ?

"Maybe they're just super famous and trying to hide from the paparazzi?" I squeaked out hopefully.

"Oh, *por favor.*" Feye rolled his eyes. "You know that makes no sense, A."

"Shhh. They might hear you."

"Let's just say hello and then keep moving," Feye said. He looked so small compared to the grown man, and I wondered if we were in more trouble than we could get out of, for once. The boats were now close enough that we could shout to the very big, non-touristy, and non-famous-looking adults.

But the man did still look familiar . . . Where had I seen him before? Duke, who had been next to us, glaring at the incoming boat in silence, let out a deep growl and began barking again.

"Oi! You two kids all right?" the man said in a deep voice.

He took off his sunglasses to look at us, and it suddenly hit me where I recognized him from—these were the poachers I had seen in town! How could I warn Feye? Now that we were up close, I could see their black hats had a symbol stitched in gray on the front. It looked sort of like an overlapping net and a fishing lure.

Feye stood away from the dinghy's engine and nodded. "Yes, sir. My little sister just forgot her field notebook the other day and came back to get it.

Right, A?" He looked back at me and silently nodded at my pocket. I bent my head down, scared, and then looked at the pocket he was motioning to. It was then that I remembered Mr. Savage's notebook was in my pocket!

"Yes! Here it is!" I exclaimed, and took the field notebook out of my back pocket, waving the bright thing in the air. *Please let them find this convincing.* "It fell out of the boat while I was taking photos. My brother was super nice to bring me back," I continued to fib.

Their boat drifted closer to us, and Duke started barking again. Were they going to let us pass by them? Or were we trapped?

CHAPTER TWENTY

Suddenly, we heard a megaphone squeal. "Hey, kids! You all right?" we heard a voice boom. It was Connor!

I had never been so happy to hear an Australian accent in my life! I stood up and waved as a third boat entered the channel. Inside it were some of our crew members, cameras in their hands, pointed right at us. I looked back to Feye, who had relief written all over his face. Even Duke seemed relieved, back to his happy barking!

I turned to look at the poachers. The man put his hat and sunglasses back on and the woman pulled her hat down over her face more. It was as if they didn't want to be seen.

"What are you guys doing here?" Connor yelled to us. "I didn't see you or Duke around and had wondered where you had gone!" It was then that Connor acknowledged the other boat. "Err . . . hello. Thanks for finding them," he said to the couple.

"Pleasure," the man said. He revved their engine and their boat roared back to life.

Connor turned his attention back to us. "Do I want to know?"

I smiled at him. "It's a long story."

"How did you find us?" Feye asked. Connor pointed at Duke, who was now watching him and wagging his tail.

"Duke's barking," Connor explained. "We were coming out here to film some sunset action in the mangroves when we heard him. It sounded different, meaner than usual, so we thought you guys might be in trouble."

"Well, it is a good thing you came when you did," I said. I pointed to the cooler. "We figured out the crocodile was a mom and so we just had to come back for her eggs. And we found them!"

"We should get back. Before Mom and Dad get too worried," Feye said.

Connor nodded. "We'll see you guys later. Going to try to shoot some footage now."

"Thank you! Good luck!" Feye said. His knuckles were white on the handle of the dinghy's steering stick. He was still scared . . . and to be honest, so was I.

Feye turned the engine back on and made his way slowly down the path we had come from. When we were far enough from the crew's boat, Feye sped the dinghy up. Duke settled down at his feet and closed his eyes. I moved back to be closer to them both, bending down to pet Duke and tell him how much of a good boy he was. Soon, we were zipping back down the channel, the dread in our stomachs still weighing heavy.

CHAPTER TWENTY-ONE

Once I finished helping Feye tie the dinghy to the docking station, I grabbed the cooler containing the crocodile eggs and handed it to Feye. He quickly placed it on the ground and gave me a helping hand up.

"Is your leg doing okay?" he asked, wiping sweat from his forehead with the end of his shirt. Mom hated when he did that, and she would've talked his ear off if she had seen him do it. I nodded and let loose a sigh of relief. We were back at the home base, safe, and away from those creepy poachers.

Duke jumped out of the boat and ran in the

direction of our rooms. Someone was ready for a rest. He had earned it! I handed Feye Mr. Savage's notebook and he put it in his back pocket.

"You snoop and see what he wrote?" Feye joked.

I shook my head. "No. To be honest, I've been scared since we left that channel and was just focused on getting back safe." Feye nodded and turned toward the cooler full of eggs.

"Need help?" he asked, pointing to it.

"No, it isn't too heavy. But can you go ahead of me and see where Mom and Dad are?" I asked, bending down to grab the handles of the cooler. With a heave, I balanced the cooler on my good leg and pulled the cooler up. We made our way to the last place we had seen our parents, by the large crocodile container, but they weren't there. In fact, no one was there. The table where the crew had been watching that day's film was now gone, as was the extra equipment that had been lying around.

"Maybe they're in their room?" Feye suggested.

"How about that room?" I said, jutting out my chin to point to the closed door under the stairs. Feye was about to open the heavy door when we heard a familiar voice shout, "There you are!" from above us.

There was no confusing that voice. It was Mr. Savage. He was wearing a black hat, black sunglasses, and a white shirt that said PRODUCER across the front.

"Mr. Savage, you're never going to believe what we found!" Feye called up, beaming. He pointed to the mud-covered cooler in my arms.

"What do you have there?" Mr. Savage asked. He came down and peered at the container, his nose wrinkling from the smell. We weren't exactly clean-looking, and we knew we reeked of mangrove mud . . . which sort of smelled like rotten eggs. Mangrove fruit decomposes in the hot Cuban sun, producing hydrogen sulfide gas—that was why the whole area smelled like rotten eggs or sewage. He stood back a bit, probably not wanting to get the smelly mud on his clean clothes. Mangrove mud didn't come off easily.

"Crocodile eggs! The injured female crocodile is a mother!" Feye explained. He opened the lid of the cooler, and the white eggs were clearly visible through the dark mud.

Mr. Savage let out a small gasp.

"And we got some great footage of—" Feye began, but I suddenly shoved him. I wasn't sure why, but I didn't want to tell Mr. Savage about our run-in with the Mega Croc just yet. Feye glared at me, but I just shook my head.

"Footage of what?" Mr. Savage asked.

"A cool boa we saw," I lied.

"Splendid! Well, let's focus on this grand discovery here, kids. We may not have the Mega Croc footage we needed, but this discovery might just be our saving grace." He went to reach for the cooler when Feye suddenly patted his pockets.

"Oh! Mr. Savage, I think this belongs to you," Feye said, pulling the bright yellow notebook out of his pocket. He handed it to Mr. Savage, who smiled widely.

"Thank you. Now how about giving me that heavy cooler before you hurt yourself?" He bent down to grab the cooler from me, but I moved away.

"Um, it's okay, Mr. Savage, I can hold on to them!" I said, trying to keep him from taking the cooler. I was slippery from the mud and I almost dropped it.

"Nonsense, it's clearly too heavy for you, and we don't want you putting more weight than you have to on that leg of yours! Let me take it from you, Adrianna," he said. But he didn't sound as friendly anymore. I got a bad feeling in my stomach, the same one I'd had in the mangroves when we saw those strangers.

The squeak of a door opening distracted us all.

"*Mi tesoro*, what do you have there?" Dad asked me, staring at the muddy cooler we were playing tug-of-war with. I turned to look at him and lifted the cooler up a little bit.

"Crocodile eggs! Feye and I figured out she was a mother. We can't leave her eggs behind," I said proudly. The eggs would be safe with Dad.

Dad looked surprised and took the lid off the cooler. "Well, I'll be . . ." he breathed. He put the lid back on and took the cooler out of our hands, then ushered us toward the room where the rest of the film crew was.

"Julio, allow me to—" Mr. Savage began to tell Dad, arms reaching out to grab the cooler back. But Dad interrupted him, gesturing for him to enter the room before him.

"Nonsense, Rick, the cooler isn't heavy, and it is in good hands," our dad said.

Safe. The eggs were safe. I smiled to myself. After a few seconds of Mr. Savage not moving, Dad shrugged his shoulders and went ahead of him.

"Seems the kids are detectives and cracked a case while we were busy getting ready to go home to the sanctuary with the injured croc," he announced to the group. The lingering boat employees came to crowd around the cooler, now placed on a seat. Feye reached over and took the lid off once more, pointing out the eggs in the mud.

"There are over thirty eggs!" he said, smiling. A female American crocodile typically lays a clutch of between thirty and sixty eggs, so this was a small batch.

"You guys went alone to get these? Who took you to the channel?" our mom asked.

Uh-oh. We knew that tone—we were in trouble. Before I could say anything, my older brother jumped in. "I'm sorry, Mom, but we didn't want to bother you guys. And Adrianna really wanted to see some more of the mangroves before we left."

"You went out *alone*?" Mr. Savage asked from the doorway. His voice startled me. He must have silently entered the room behind us.

"We weren't that far away," I said. "And we saw Connor and some of the film crew while we were out."

Mr. Savage shook his head. Mom mirrored his movements, arms crossing in front of her chest.

"Where are they?" Mr. Savage asked.

"Filming some sunset shots," Feye said, uncertainty in his voice. Mr. Savage grumbled something under his breath that I couldn't understand.

"I'd like for you all to give us a few minutes," Mom said, and looked around at the people in the room. They quickly left—even they were afraid of my mom's angry expression.

CHAPTER TWENTY-TWO

"You could've gotten lost, run out of fuel, gotten into an accident, or worse—run into some bad people!" Mom said. "These mangroves are not safe for two kids to wander around all alone."

Feye hung his head low, avoiding looking at our mother. Now it was my turn to speak for us.

"Mom, we just wanted to help. We knew you were all busy, and we didn't want to bother you. We wanted to show how responsible we could be, too," I said. Our mother leaned in close and gave us both a big hug. Feye and I looked at each other, pressed against our mother's chest, surprised. We were expecting her to yell at us, not give us a hug!

"Do not do that again. Understand?" Dad said, arms crossed in front of him. "You're grounded, and we will be talking about your appearances on the show with Mr. Savage."

We bowed our heads and nodded.

Mom turned toward us. "While we don't agree with how you went about everything, we *are* proud of you for figuring out that she had laid eggs. You really helped her out. I don't know if you know this, but American crocodiles are actually listed as Vulnerable by the IUCN," she said.

"What's the IUCN?" Feye asked.

"IUCN stands for the International Union for Conservation of Nature. It's the world's oldest environmental organization. Their job is to tell scientists and conservationists, like us, how animals and plants are doing. Are their populations okay? Do they need better protection?" Dad explained, pulling up the IUCN website on his tablet. He showed us different animals like sharks, elephants, lions, sea turtles, and even some species of mice. Each said "Vulnerable," "Endangered," or "Extinct in the Wild."

Dad took the tablet once again and typed something into the website. Up came a picture of the American crocodile with what I recognized as the scientific name underneath: *Crocodylus acutus*. It said VULNERABLE in big letters.

"What does Vulnerable mean for the crocodiles?" I asked.

"Vulnerable for any animal means that the IUCN thinks they will become endangered unless scientists and other people can help them out," Mom said. "That means we need to protect them. Usually an animal gets the label Vulnerable because people have destroyed their habitat or hunted them too much."

GREEN SEA TURTLE

- The Green Sea Turtle gets its name not from its outward appearance, but from the fat stores inside its body–the fat is greenish in color!
- A healthy sea turtle can live up to 100 years!
- In the last fifty years, the sea turtle population has decreased over 90 percent, due to things like climate change and loss of habitat.

"American crocodiles have lost a lot of their homes due to humans," she continued. "So zoos all over the world, like ours, have breeding programs. That means we help the crocodiles get together and make babies. In some places, people actually steal crocodile eggs, too, so these are very important to keep. We'll be able to help them hatch safely. That will help their numbers here."

"So does that mean we will have more than thirty crocodiles at the zoo? That's a lot of mouths to feed!" Feye looked on, a bit horrified. He helped cut up the food for the big crocodiles and was probably thinking of all the extra work he would have to do.

Mom and Dad laughed, shaking their heads. "We'll figure that out once we're home and at the zoo. But we definitely won't keep all of them. Some may go to other zoos, while the others will get released back out into the wild," Mom said.

"How will we know if the babies make it?" I asked, wondering if we could ever come back to Cuba and say hi to them.

"We're going to put tracking tags on the ones we release back into the wild," Dad replied. "That way we can see where they go! If we get the funding for it, we might be able to come here once a year with crocodile scientists and measure how big they have gotten and how many are still around. We can talk about it with a few friends when we get back home." Dad looked at Mom, who nodded in agreement.

The next morning, we all sat at breakfast in silence, enjoying the sights and sounds of the mangrove forest through the boat hotel's windows for the last time.

Mr. Savage knocked on the door and cleared his throat. "All right, Villalobos family. Pack up your things. The boat to take us inland will be arriving shortly. We've got a long day ahead of us to get this croc and her eggs back to Sacred Sanctuary and Zoological Park." He opened the door behind him widely so we could all get out and up to our rooms to finish packing.

When I was done, I picked up Duke and walked over to Connor.

"Should we try to find someone willing to adopt Duke? I want to bring him back, but my parents won't let me." I could feel tears welling up in my eyes.

"Don't worry, Adrianna. I'll take care of Duke, okay?" Connor said.

"Just promise me that he won't end up on the streets or in a pound."

"I promise," Connor said, and coaxed Duke from my arms.

The rest of the team would join us back home in the next few days. With hugs all around to the Cuban film crew, and a final pet and scratch for

Duke, we stepped into the boat and drove away from the mangroves one last time. I looked down into the crocodile holding container and smiled, glad we had rescued this mama.

The boat ride wasn't too long, and I spent most of it staring at the blue shades in the water. Every now and then a flying fish would soar next to our boat wake, frightened by the noise and possibly saying hello. Just in case they were saying hello, I waved to every single one I saw.

Feye came to sit down next to me. "Why'd you stop me from telling Mr. Savage about the footage we took of that massive croc? Did you want all the credit or something?"

"No, no, I—"

"You don't have to keep trying to prove yourself to everyone, you know. Mom and Dad might be worried about your safety, but you did a lot of things right and really showed you have what it takes to be a part of this show."

I smiled at the compliment, nudging him as a thanks. But that wasn't the reason at all.

"How many really big crocodiles are out there, Feye? They're a Vulnerable species. So it's our responsibility to protect the big ones, like this so-called 'Mega Croc,' whenever we can." I took a deep breath. "I don't think we should give the footage over to Mr. Savage."

"What! But the show is in jeopardy!" argued Feye.

"I don't think it is anymore. Mr. Savage said that the production team had enough drama to work with, now that we have the eggs. And there's lots of other stuff, too—the mistake I made with the tag, my bite, us finding the injured croc! If we give the Mega Croc footage to Mr. Savage, we could possibly lead the poachers right to where we found it. Or a bunch of new ones, even. Any of them could end up killing the Mega Croc!"

Feye didn't say anything, but he looked thoughtful.

"We always say keeping wildlife safe and helping animals is what we love doing most. So, let's do that," I said. "We don't need a TV show to prove anything."

"But the TV show lets us help even more animals," Feye countered.

"Not like this! Not by showing poachers where rare and special animals like the Mega Croc are."

That got through to Feye. He nodded and pulled out his phone. Together we deleted the footage.

CHAPTER TWENTY-THREE

The sound of kookaburras greeted me as I opened the car door and jumped out into the hot, summer day. Out of all the birds we housed, the kookaburras had to be the loudest.

I yawned and wiped some of the sleep from my eyes, then stretched my arms upward. As Mom and Dad closed their car doors, we all made our way to the back gates of Sacred Sanctuary and Zoological Park to start our day.

It had been a month since we returned from Cuba with the injured female crocodile and her eggs. Once we had reached Sacred Sanctuary, we called on one of our reptile experts to show us how to tell whether the crocodile eggs were fertilized or not. We found out that they all contained baby crocodiles, and all of them had hatched shortly after.

It was up to Feye, Alessi, and me to cut up their meals and feed them. Half of them would be going to other zoos to help with their breeding programs, while the other half would be going back into the wild.

In a few days, we'd return to Cuba to release those hatchlings back to their home. We'd named the mother crocodile Luz, which means "light" in Spanish. She'd made a full recovery from her injuries and was going back out with them. The producers loved the dramatics of our show, and the happy ending, and had given us the "green light" for more episodes in the future!

The tagged crocodile, who Feye decided to name Terminator, was still pinging away even after all this time, too! My parents and the local Cuban crocodile scientists had been keeping up with his movements in the mangroves to see where he spent the most time. Maybe he and Luz would cross paths.

As Feye cut up the crocodiles' meat, I took white vitamin pills and shoved them into the center of each piece. Since we were getting ready to release them into the wild, we wanted to make sure the hatchlings were as healthy as possible in order to have the best chance out there. Our lead veterinarian, Dr. Jay Cruz, had figured out the exact amount of vitamins each baby and their mom needed. She was one of my favorite people at the Wildlife Hospital because she didn't think of me as too young to learn about vet science.

This had to be my favorite part of our job: Getting to take care of the animals, learn about them, and teach people about them and the dangers they face out in the wild is the coolest thing. I had gotten to spend a lot of time with the hatchlings, learning to tell them apart by their different colors and spots.

My favorite was the smallest baby crocodile we had, who was a stunning bright green color. I called her Isabella. She always let me pick her up without ever trying to bite me, even in the very beginning, and she tended to follow me around whatever enclosure we were in when she thought I had food.

"Hey, guys, sorry to interrupt. We've got a group to see Adrianna's croc bite talk in about five minutes. A, are you good to go?" Mom asked.

I nodded and put the rest of the meat down and in the steel bucket. I moved over to the sink and washed my hands with soap and hot water and quickly changed into my khaki shorts.

"Ready to go!" I said.

Connor put a microphone headset on me that wrapped around my ears, and he smiled at me. I wore this whenever I went out into the croc rehabilitation center so the audience could hear me. We quickly tested it to make sure it was working fine, but were interrupted by Duke's barking.

Connor had ended up adopting Duke, and now he comes in to work with him all the time! So, it's sort of like Feye and I have our own dog. After a quick pet for Duke, I grabbed the steel buckets full of cut-up meat and went to the back exit of the hospital that led into the croc zone.

I could hear my dad announce me before the door to the croc zone even opened. When it did open, for a second I couldn't see any of the people who looked down into the arena. With over thirty baby crocodiles that were now about half the size of my arm, we'd had to build a big enclosure to fit all of them! Along with a bunch of professional artists, Feye and I had painted the walls of the enclosure to look like a mangrove forest, the roots of the painted trees disappearing under the sand we had filled the bottom of the enclosure with.

We had a giant saltwater lake on one side of the enclosure, where the baby crocodiles could swim and hunt for live fish. My favorite part was having a bubble made of really tough glass in the center of the whole thing that you could squeeze into and see the crocodiles swimming around you underwater. I had played hide-and-seek with many of the baby crocs, but especially Isabella, in that bubble. I would miss seeing them there all the time!

There were two main areas where people could see the crocodiles. One was closer to the enclosure itself, where we had a walkabout canopy made of wood. From there, viewers could get a bird's eye view of the crocodiles. The canopy led into the second area, our Wildlife Café, where people could eat, look out at the view from Sacred Sanctuary and Zoological Park, or look down into the enclosure and see the shows. Both parts were packed with people, ready to hear me talk!

"*Hola!* How are we doing today?" I said into the microphone, waving one hand up in the air while the other was holding on to both of the steel buckets. The audience roared back a hello, and I smiled. This was one of the coolest parts of my job here at the park, getting to talk to people about the amazing animals we have.

"I'm really lucky to be here today to talk to you all about the American crocodile, many of whom are all around my feet and clearly know I have food." I laughed as they began to crawl over my feet and try to climb up my leg. I gently shook them off and began to walk to the middle of the enclosure. "They are a species of crocodile that lives in North and South America, including the Caribbean, where we found these little ones!" I put my bucket down on a ledge too high for the baby crocodiles to reach with their little snouts. I looked around to find Isabella, who was easy to spot since she was so bright green. I was the saddest to see her leave. She'd be going to a zoo in Canada to hopefully one day become a mom herself.

I picked her up for a quick second as I explained all about the crocodiles' anatomy and then put her down when she got super wriggly. She was very patient, but she knew food was nearby and she wanted it *now.* I laughed and reached into my bucket and put a piece of meat in front of her, which she quickly gobbled up. Crocodiles mainly eat fish, but some of the larger ones eat other kinds of meat like deer or chicken. So we fed the baby crocodiles a mixture of fish and chicken so they didn't get bored.

I heard a lot of oohs and aahs as I quickly put meat down in certain places around the arena and had the baby crocs follow me around to find it. When I ran out of meat from one bucket, I grabbed the other one that was safely away from their little mouths and did the same thing. The audience clapped and took pictures.

"Those teeth can cut through muscle and bone very easily! When they grow up, they can take on some pretty big animals. They are famous for their 'death roll,' where they get a chunk of meat in their jaws and spin around," I said, pointing to the screens around the enclosure, which now showed Luz performing the famous death roll.

Some people let out a loud gasp. I pointed to my leg, where you could see yellow bruising, bright purple scars, and some Band-Aids. "I know more than anyone how scared someone can be of crocodiles. A month ago, I was bitten and dragged by a large crocodile while filming for our show. I don't blame the crocodile at all. I was a visitor in its home, and it just took a nibble to figure out what I was. This is called an exploratory bite, and other animals, like sharks, do it, too!" I had told this story so many times that to me it felt just like that—a story. I hadn't had any nightmares of that night, but I was still uneasy about swimming at night or being in murky water. Sometimes I forgot the bite had happened at all until I looked down at my leg or something brushed up against it and it hurt.

"A lot of people say I should be afraid of crocodiles after this happened, but honestly? I'm not. We should be afraid for the crocodiles, not of them. People hunt them for their skin and their eggs, and we are also ruining their homes. They are an important part of the environment, and I hope that by showing you that I, a person who got bit by one, am not afraid of them . . . then maybe you won't be either." I saw many people nodding, and a thunderous applause erupted from the crowd.

A scratch on my leg made me look down to see Isabella trying to get my attention. When she saw she had it, her mouth opened wide. Ha! She wanted more food. I laughed, bowed my head down, and waved with both of my hands to say goodbye to the crowd but also to show the baby crocs I had no more food. "That's all from me today, everyone! Thank you so much for coming to Sacred Sanctuary and Zoological Park!" Isabella was still waiting, mouth open, not getting the hint that the show was over.

I picked her up with one hand and cradled her in my arms for a few seconds, running my hand down her back as my own way to say goodbye. She got wriggly once more, so I put her down and waved to the crowd for another minute before heading back through the door I'd come through. Feye gave me a big high five and Dad and Mom hugged me. I looked back at the door, now shut, and smiled. I love this job—and I couldn't wait to get back out there to rescue some more animals!

AUTHOR'S NOTE

Did you know that the author (that's me!) was actually bitten and dragged by a crocodile, just like Adrianna? I was diving underwater while filming for a TV show about hammerhead sharks in Cuba.

At the end of one of my dives, my dive mask started acting up, just like Adrianna's. The microphone cut off, meaning I couldn't hear the crew, and they couldn't hear me. So when my dive buddy gave me the hand signal to start heading up, I was relieved. He started floating up. Not wanting to get hit with his swimming fins, I waited a few seconds before following him. It was in these few seconds that an American crocodile bit down on my leg and starting to drag me backward through the water.

I did my best to stay calm. I knew that the most important thing was not to move my leg, or to struggle. A crocodile's mouth is highly receptive to texture and taste. I didn't feel pain, just pressure. So I was hoping that the crocodile was only tasting the neoprene of my suit, not my actual leg. If it decided that scuba suit wasn't food, it would hopefully release its jaws and let me go.

Finally, it did! I was able to swim to the surface and get medical attention for the bite. When an animal tastes a potential food like this, it's called an "exploratory bite." The crocodile was exploring whether or not this new object might be edible. Fortunately, the croc decided that I wasn't! Adrianna and I have matching scars—an imprint of a crocodile jaw on the inside of our left leg and two puncture wounds on the outside of that leg.

Although there were a lot of safety measures in place for the filming and everyone followed directions—just like you see in the book—accidents can still happen! Similarly to Adrianna, I don't blame the crew or the crocodile for what happened. I want to give a big shout-out to the medics who took amazing care of me: Mike Hudson and Yusniel Soriano Aguero.

ALLIGATOR VS. CROCODILE: WHAT'S THE DIFFERENCE?

·**SNOUT SHAPE:** Alligators have wider, U-shaped snouts while crocodile snouts are more pointed and V-shaped.

·**TOOTHY GRIN:** When their snouts are shut, crocodiles have teeth that stick out. For alligators, all their teeth are hidden because their top jaw is wider than their lower one. Crocodiles win for bite strength—they have a bite pressure that measures 3,700 pounds per square inch. The strongest alligators' bites are about 2,900 pounds per square inch.

·**HOME BASE:** Crocodiles like to live in saltwater habitats, while alligators hang out in freshwater marshes and lakes. Alligators can tolerate cold weather better than crocodiles.

·**SIZE:** An adult crocodile can grow up to roughly 19 feet long; the maximum length for an alligator is around 14 feet.

·LOOKS: Crocodiles tend to be more of a light tan or olive color, whereas alligators are usually a dark black gray.

·ON LAND: Both crocodiles and alligators can move quickly on land for short distances. They can both "gallop" or "sprint" but only do it when threatened. A crocodile might reach almost 9 miles per hour (14 kilometers per hour) while an alligator might reach a maximum speed of about 11 miles per hour (18 kilometers per hour).

·IN WATER: Both crocodiles and alligators move much faster in the water than on land because they can use their long, muscular tails to propel their bodies through the water. When crocodiles swim, they might reach speeds of about 9 miles per hour (15 kilometers per hour) while alligators are much faster and might reach a maximum of 20 miles per hour (32 kilometers per hour). These speeds are for short bursts of energy.

AMERICAN CROCODILE FACTS
(CROCODYLUS ACUTUS)

The scientific name means "pointy-snouted crocodile."

- **TYPE OF ANIMAL:** Reptile.
- **WHERE YOU CAN FIND IT:** Lives from the southern United States to northern South America.
- **WHAT IT EATS:** Feeds on mostly fish but can feed on small mammals, birds, crabs, insects, snails, frogs, and even deer!
- **AVERAGE LIFE SPAN IN THE WILD:** 70 years.
- **SIZE:** Up to 15 feet (4.6 meters). They are among the largest of the world's crocodiles!
- **WEIGHT:** Up to 2,000 pounds (907.2 kilograms).
- **INTERNATIONAL UNION FOR CONSERVATION OF NATURE (IUCN) RED LIST STATUS:** Vulnerable.
- **CONSERVATION STATUS:** Most countries in the American crocodile's range have passed protection laws, but few governments enforce these laws. A lot of illegal

hunting and habitat loss have hurt the American crocodile population!

WHAT TO DO IF YOU ENCOUNTER A CROCODILE IN THE WILD

Crocodiles have been known to bite people but are far more likely to flee at the sight of humans.

STAY AWAY.

If you can see the crocodile from far away, make sure to keep your distance. Never, ever feed crocodiles! If you think you are somewhere that has crocodiles or if there's a sign warning of crocodiles in the area, stay at least 20 feet away from the water (recommended by the National Park Service).

GET OUT OF THE WATER.

Crocodiles naturally attack and kill their prey in the water, since they are masters of staying quiet and hidden until it is too late. If you are on a boat in water that has crocodiles, keep your arms and legs inside the boat at all times. Do not swim in water that has a sign warning of crocodiles in the area.

RUN.

If you see a crocodile on land, run as fast as you can! Crocodiles can run at a maximum speed of around 9 miles per hour, and they can do this for only a short time. Although there's a myth that running in a zigzag can keep you safe, the truth is that it doesn't matter if you run straight or in a zigzag—just make sure you keep running.

LEARN SPANISH WITH THE VILLALOBOS FAMILY!

- ¡Un año más! = One more year!
- Aves de Cuba = Birds of Cuba
- ¿Donde están tus modales? = Where are your manners?
- ¿Están ustedes allí? = Are you guys there?
- ¡Vemos un cocodrilo! = We see a crocodile!
- Muchachos = Boys
- Lo siento mucho = I'm so sorry
- ¡Hola familia Villalobos! = Hello, Villalobos family!
- Mi amigo = My friend
- Familia = Family
- Bienvenidos = Welcome
- Gracias = Thank you
- Mi nena = My girl (or daughter)
- Satos = Mutts
- ¡Oye! ¡Regresa aquí! = Hey! Get back here!
- Empleado de la perrera = Dogcatcher
- Hola pequeña. ¿Ese es tu perro? = Hello, little girl. Is this your dog?

- Es mío = He's mine
- Cuídate = Take care of yourself
- Tienda = Store
- La perrera = The dog pound
- Mijo = My son
- Mija = My daughter
- ¡Estamos listos! = We're ready
- Mi amor = My love
- Mijos = My kids/my children
- Señorita = Little miss
- Azul = Blue
- Basta = Stop
- Vamonos = Let's go
- Nada = Nothing
- Por favor = Please
- Mi tesoro = My treasure
- Hola = Hello

DON'T MISS ADRIANNA'S NEXT ADVENTURE!

Author photo by Connor Watling

Known as the "Mother of Sharks," Melissa Cristina Márquez is a Latina marine biologist who has a lot of labels: science communicator, conservationist, author, educator, podcaster, and television presenter. Born in Puerto Rico and raised all over the world, she now calls Australia home. She studies sharks, climbs up sand dunes, spies on birds in the rain forest, and tracks down kangaroos in the Outback . . . and then writes about her adventures! *Wild Survival: Crocodile Rescue!* is her debut novel. Find Melissa online at melissacristinamarquez.com.